He was Here to Harass the Barringtons.

Alex vowed silently that she'd ignore this man's physical appeal and never see him again. She couldn't afford to befriend someone who was out to destroy the Barringtons—who, in turn, could easily destroy her.

"Why don't you forget the muckraking journalism and write a novel instead? Your hero could live on an ancient boat with his only companion—his faithful dog."

"Hey, now that's an idea," Will declared. "Everybody loves dog stories."

"You could call it *Man's Best Friend.*"

"Well now, much as I love dogs in general, and mine in particular, my own personal belief has always been that man's best friend is . . . woman."

AMANDA YORK

was born and raised in Liverpool, England, where she married an American airman and proceeded to fall in love with his country. They have two sons and a daughter, of whom they're incredibly proud. When not writing, she loves physical activities—but there's always a story simmering on the back burner.

Dear Reader:

SILHOUETTE DESIRE is an exciting new line of contemporary romances from Silhouette Books. During the past year, many Silhouette readers have written in telling us what other types of stories they'd like to read from Silhouette, and we've kept these comments and suggestions in mind in developing SILHOUETTE DESIRE.

DESIREs feature all of the elements you like to see in a romance, plus a more sensual, provocative story. So if you want to experience all the excitement, passion and joy of falling in love, then SILHOUETTE DESIRE is for you.

Karen Solem
Editor-in-Chief
Silhouette Books

AMANDA YORK
Man's Best Friend

Silhouette Desire

Published by Silhouette Books New York

America's Publisher of Contemporary Romance

Silhouette Books by Amanda York

An Old-Fashioned Love (IM# 56)
Man's Best Friend (DES# 205)

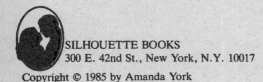
SILHOUETTE BOOKS
300 E. 42nd St., New York, N.Y. 10017

Copyright © 1985 by Amanda York

Distributed by Pocket Books

ISBN: 0-373-05205-7

First Silhouette Books printing May, 1985

10 9 8 7 6 5 4 3 2 1

Man's
Best Friend

1

The strange dog appeared out of the mist so suddenly that a sandpiper fluttered aloft, shrieking in fright. Red Baron stopped investigating a scurrying sand crab and raised his aristocratic head to stare in amazement.

Alex skidded to a halt, cold seawater lapping at her bare feet. She called sharply, "Stay, Red!"

One glance at the soaking wet and disheveled Golden Retriever suggested that some cruel owner had abandoned him, perhaps even tossed him out of a passing boat, since this tiny cove was inaccessible from the rocky bluff, except by means of the steps cut into the cliff from Alex's cottage.

She extended her hand toward the retriever, murmuring, "Hi, boy, easy boy, we won't hurt you." He wagged his tail, cocked his head on one side and gave Red Baron an interested stare.

Red Baron approached the intruder carefully, tail erect

so that his championship feathers were carried like an Indian chief's headdress. Alex said again, "Stay. No, Red, come back."

But for once Red Baron's good manners were forgotten. The two dogs nuzzled one another joyfully, then raced off into the swirling mist.

Damn! She'd be late opening the office and Mrs. Barrington was bringing in her Chinese Shar-pei at nine. As far as the Barringtons were concerned, Alex's taking over of the only veterinary practice in town was still in its trial phase, despite Rodney Barrington's interest in Alex, which she suspected was simply an addiction to slender blondes. The Barringtons owned the bank which carried Alex's loan, the only newspaper in Sand Point and huge hunks of real estate. Bart Barrington, Rodney's father, was also a congressman. Nobody kept Amelia Barrington waiting. Least of all the old veterinarian's female assistant, who'd had the audacity to take what the Barringtons considered to be a man's job.

Stumbling over the wet sand in pursuit of Red Baron, Alex called frantically, but futilely for her Irish Setter to return. She caught a quick glimpse of a feathered red tail disappearing into a denser patch of fog at the same instant she heard a boat scraping up on the beach.

Alex felt an uneasy pang. Nobody ever put in to what she had come to regard as her private cove. The tiny crescent of beach was locked in by rocks and often lashed by high surf, making beaching a boat a dangerous maneuver.

Forgetting the dogs for a moment, Alex turned to see the misty shape of a man stepping from a weather-beaten wooden dinghy. A big man, with powerful shoulders straining the threadbare Aran sweater he wore over

8

salt-caked jeans. Tousled hair, sandy flecked with red, topped a face that even a mother couldn't have described as handsome, but Alex noted as he came closer his features had an appealing rugged vitality and a certain searching inquisitiveness in the eyes. But the overall impression he gave was that of a man who cared little about his appearance. Unshaven, uncombed, definitely untidy.

"'Morning, ma'am. Hope I didn't startle you. I didn't think anybody would be about this early in the morning." The voice matched the face, deep, resonant, with an anticipatory lilt to it as though its owner expected an intriguing response.

"I take it that you're looking for your dog," Alex said coldly, thinking that from what she'd seen of the condition of the Golden Retriever's coat, both dog and owner were equally disreputable-looking.

"Yes, ma'am. Meggie jumped overboard before I could stop her. I expect she was getting cabin-fever, cooped up with me aboard the boat. I've a twenty-five-foot sloop—"

"*Meggie?*" Alex interrupted. "The retriever is a female? Oh, God no! She's not in heat?"

"Well, as a matter of fact—"

"You irresponsible idiot! How can you let a purebred run loose when she's in heat?" The words were flung over Alex's shoulder as she turned and raced in the direction she had seen the two dogs take.

She heard the man's footsteps, muffled by the sand, behind her. They ran in circles, calling to their dogs, until the rising sun made inroads into the sea mist and Alex caught sight of the flurry of red and gold in the shelter of the tide pools by the water's edge.

Furious, Alex jumped onto the moss-covered rocks recently exposed by the ebb tide, and promptly lost her balance. For a split second she clawed at the air, then plunged into an icy pool of water.

The pool was only waist deep, but Alex was wet from head to toe. Coughing and spitting saltwater, she stood up, her hair streaming in long dripping tendrils down her face.

Expertly balancing tattered sneakers on the rock, the stranger tried unsuccessfully to hide his grin as he extended his hand to help her out. But Alex ignored it, staring with horrified fascination as Red Baron, his brown velvet eyes rolling in ecstasy, prepared to consummate the act of procreation with an equally enthusiastic Golden Retriever.

"Stop them!" Alex screamed. "Hurry, separate them. They can't . . . they mustn't . . . oh, good lord, don't stand there. Do something."

The untidy man glanced back at the two dogs, hand still held toward Alex. "Ma'am, I believe it's too late."

Alex grabbed his hand and he pulled her up onto the rock beside him. Immediately he slipped his other hand around her waist to steady her on the slippery surface.

"Let go of me, you fool. Don't you see what's happening? My dog is . . . is . . ."

"Making love to mine. Yes, I see that. It's really quite beautiful, isn't it?" He had brown eyes, crinkling now with both amusement and patient acceptance of the situation. Why, Alex thought, more angry than ever, he's completely unconcerned that his Golden Retriever is mating with a different breed of dog.

Several possibilities flashed through Alex's mind as she

jerked free of his grasp and made her way cautiously toward the dogs. Perhaps when he learned she was a veterinarian, he'd sue her for allowing her dog to sully his. Perhaps the dog wasn't his? Perhaps he'd stolen it? How could the owner of a purebred be so casual, under the circumstances? Even though his Meggie was in a disgraceful state of grooming, it was obvious that she was a valuable animal.

She circled the two dogs, trying to grab Red Baron, but it was useless. The act was complete. Alex let out her breath in an exasperated sigh. Her experienced eye told her that Meggie had not yet had a litter, which meant to some people who still subscribed to the old wives' tale that she was now ruined, since she would probably give birth to mongrel pups. Still, perhaps her owner wasn't aware that the old myth persisted.

He strolled over to her and looked down at the two panting dogs. "My name's Will O'Keefe, ma'am. And this is Meggie." There was mock seriousness in his voice, but from the look in his eyes laughter might come rumbling out of him at any second.

"Alex Aimes. I'm a practicing veterinarian. If she is pregnant I can take care of that without charge, of course. A responsible owner would have her spayed anyway if they weren't planning on breeding her and couldn't adequately protect her when she was in heat. I can take care of both problems simultaneously if you want. When can you bring her into my surgery?"

Will O'Keefe raised a shaggy eyebrow. "Why, Alex—"

"*Doctor* Aimes."

"Alex," he repeated firmly. "I wouldn't dream of forcing Meggie to have an abortion. If she fell in love with

11

your dog, that's fine by me. Meggie's my friend. I'll take care of her and any puppies she has."

Alex was speechless. "That is the most irresponsible, childishly stupid thing I ever heard." Despite her tirade, she felt a small, unwanted, glimmer of admiration for a man so obviously devoted to his dog. If she had time, and Mrs. Barrington were not waiting for her, perhaps he would listen to reason and she could convince him she merely wanted to act in the best interests of his pet.

He gave her an apologetic so-be-it grin that said she was probably right but he had his principles too.

To cover her momentary lapse of righteous indignation, Alex added in as businesslike tone as she could muster, "When you come to your senses you can bring her in to see me—I'm the only veterinarian in Sand Point. Now, will you please get yourself and your dog off my beach at once?"

"*Your* beach? You haven't heard that beyond the mean high tide line the shore belongs to everybody?"

Alex grabbed Red Baron's collar and yanked him to her. Meggie made a small sound that reminded Alex, unnervingly, of the sigh of a woman who has just experienced ecstasy. Blushing for the first time in years, Alex dragged Red Baron off to an accompanying chuckle from Will O'Keefe.

Amelia Barrington paced around the waiting room of the Sand Point Pet Hospital like a galleon under sail. Her five thousand-dollar Chinese Shar-pei, his coat more folded and creased than it seemed possible for any hide to be, lay fast asleep in an outsized satin-lined wicker basket.

Mrs. Barrington raised her plump wrist and examined

a diamond watch with elaborate care. "I have been waiting for fifteen minutes."

"I'm terribly sorry . . . something happened . . . I was delayed. A dog swam ashore from a boat."

Unnerved by her client's frosty stare, Alex found herself babbling the whole story, even though she hadn't intended to. Still, it really wasn't her fault. She and Red had been walking that little beach for months and there had never been another dog there.

"How disgusting," Mrs. Barrington commented, when she was finished. "And still another incident that proves my cause is just and timely."

Bending over the wicker basket, Alex stroked the wrinkled brow of Star of the East. "Star" to the Barringtons. He was getting far too fat. Alex decided to leave him in his basket rather than attempting to haul him into the examining room. She asked, "Your cause?"

"Didn't Rodney tell you? I want my husband to introduce a bill to pass legislation that would prohibit the indiscriminate backyard breeding of dogs. Only licensed kennels should be allowed to breed."

"Wouldn't that be a bit difficult to enforce?" Alex asked, going to the wall cabinet to find hypodermic and vaccines.

"I'm quite sure I don't have to quote statistics about the number of domestic dogs put to sleep in pounds to a veterinarian, do I?"

"No, of course not." Alex stroked Star's creased coat, smoothing out the area to receive the vaccination. Mrs. Barrington averted her gaze. She added, "There'll be an editorial in the *Bulletin* today and petitions will be circulated throughout the state."

"I do agree that something needs to be done about the

staggering number of unwanted pets, but I don't know how owner-responsibility can be legislated. It seems to me we have more laws now than it's possible to enforce."

Mrs. Barrington turned and fixed her with a rapier stare. "I shall, of course, expect your full support." She beamed down at Star of the East. "Good dog! Good boy! Did the nasty vet hurt my sweetums, then?"

Alex felt her smile congeal on her face. "He won't need any more shots now until his rabies booster."

"Go outside and get Herbert, will you, Alex? He'll have to carry poor Star—he's obviously too upset to walk to the car."

Some day, Alex thought as she went out to summon the Barrington's chauffeur, I'll hire the kind of assistant I used to be, to run interference for me with people like Amelia B.

On the street Herbert stood beside the silver Rolls-Royce, which was gleaming as the last of the morning mist was consumed by the sun. Owners of the adjacent curio shops were rolling out gaily-colored canopies and sweeping worn brick pavements. Across the street the gold-lettered sign on the window of the newspaper office proclaimed SAND POINT BULLETIN. WE PRINT THE TRUTH AND NOTHING BUT THE TRUTH.

Alex glanced down the steeply-inclined street to the bay, already dotted with fishing boats. Later, when the wind came up, there would be sails and spinnakers and the tiny town with its lovely bay would look exactly as perfect as the picture postcards depicted.

"Herbert, Mrs. Barrington wants you to go in and get Star," Alex said. The chauffeur nodded and walked stiffly toward the storefront office. Herbert was as old as God and seemed permanently bent into a driving, rather than a walking, pose.

Alex lingered, enjoying the warmth of the sun and the fresh tang of the air. A slight breeze rustled the new leaves on the silver maples lining the street and blew a strand of her hair across her eyes. She turned to shake her head and saw a man riding a battered and rusty bicycle. A broad-shouldered man in a fisherman's sweater and salt-caked jeans. Will O'Keefe, owner of the probably-pregnant Golden Retriever. He came to a stop outside the newspaper office. He hadn't lost any time in locating the veterinarian's office. There was no sign of his dog.

He jumped from the bike, swept the street with interested eyes, found Alex and saluted her, smiling. At the same instant Mrs. Barrington, preceded by Herbert carrying her Shar-pei, emerged from the pet hospital. Alex heard her gasp.

"What is it, Mrs. Barrington? Anything wrong?" Alex asked.

Mrs. Barrington was staring in apparent horror at Will O'Keefe. "That man . . . how long has he been in town? Have you seen him before?"

"Not in town, no. That's the man I was telling you about, the one who has a boat anchored in the cove. The owner of the retriever."

Will O'Keefe had leaned his bicycle against the newspaper building and was studying a front page layout on display in the window.

"Do you know him, Mrs. Barrington?" Alex asked, surprised to see that the woman's usually imperious expression had been replaced by one of unbridled fury.

"Yes," Mrs. Barrington answered, her voice a hiss like escaping steam. "He's a scoundrel, a vicious, lying, unprincipled, muckraking . . ."

Where the derogatory stream of adjectives was leading was lost to Alex as Mrs. Barrington got into the back seat of the Rolls and Herbert closed the door with a gentle thud.

2

~~~~~~~~~~~~~~~~~~~~

The Rolls was still in sight when Will crossed the street to Alex. There was now a hard look to his dark eyes. "So you're another of the Barringtons' peons. I'm disappointed."

"If you're here to make an appointment to have your dog spayed, come inside," Alex said, controlling the urge to respond with an equally insulting remark. "If not, we've nothing further to discuss."

"I do want to make an appointment," Will said, following her into the waiting room. "But not for spaying. She's got a few fleas and I guess it's time for her rabies shot."

Alex studied her appointment book. Will leaned on the counter, inches away from her. She was aware of the smell of the sea about him, pleasant and vaguely arousing. It hinted of lapping waves, lonely shores and islands hidden in the mist. The penciled names in the book blurred and she shook her head slightly, trying to reconcile Amelia Barrington's description of him with the vastly different personal impression he created. The word *physical* seemed to dance across her mind. The sheer masculine force this man exuded was almost overpowering.

To cover her confusion, Alex said, "I don't intend to charge you for spaying her, if that's the problem."

"You didn't emasculate your dog."

"Neuter is the preferred term," Alex said, feeling an unaccustomed flush stain her cheeks. "Red Baron is a championship A.K.C. Irish Setter. The kennel where I bought him wants to use him for stud purposes."

"Meg has a pedigree a mile long too."

"Then why didn't you have her mated with one of her own breed?"

Will smiled disarmingly. "Love is blind. For dogs too, I guess."

"I can fit your dog in tomorrow afternoon. If she needs flea-dipping, you should be prepared to leave her for a couple of hours."

"Fine. How about dinner tonight?"

Alex looked up. Dark brown eyes sparkled at her, reminding her uncomfortably of the way Red Baron had gazed at Meggie. Will added, "You and me, that is. Not the dogs. I'd like to make amends for causing you to fall into the sea this morning."

"That's not necessary. I accept your apology."

"Oh, I wasn't apologizing. Making amends is different."

"I'm busy tonight."

"Tomorrow? Lunch? Dinner? Late-night snack?"

"I see no point in making any kind of a social date with you, Mr. O'Keefe." She snapped the appointment book shut. "Now if you'll excuse me, I have work to do."

She went through the door into the examining room without looking back. A second door led to the indoor cages, some of which were connected to outdoor runs. A high school boy named Juan came in before and after school to feed the boarders and clean cages and pens, but Alex took care of the sick or injured animals herself.

There was only half an hour before her next appointment and Alex hurried to prepare special diets, take temperatures and still have time for soothing words to comfort her patients. Mrs. Barrington always came in before the pet hospital's nine o'clock opening, since she was afraid Star of the East might encounter another dog and be exposed to his germs. Since the Barringtons owned the building Alex leased, and the cottage in which she lived, as well as the bank carrying her loan, she didn't argue about their special requirements.

Thirty minutes later she washed her hands, pinned the errant strand of her hair back up into the topknot she wore and went back to the waiting room. Will O'Keefe was sitting reading an ancient copy of *National Geographic*. There was no sign of Alex's first patient.

"Why are you still here?" she asked. "Your dog's appointment is tomorrow afternoon."

"I forgot to ask how much it will cost—to check Meg's general health, the shot and flea-dip."

Alex glanced at his clothes, remembered the rusty bike he rode. "Suppose we say it's on the house—providing you either let me do the spaying or don't bother me again. Whichever you prefer."

He considered the offer for a moment, then rose to his feet. "I'll pay you tomorrow. I don't care for your conditions."

As he started toward the door a dark-haired little girl clutching a kitten came running across the street, tears streaming down her face. Moving with astonishing grace and speed for such a big man, Will flung open the door and intercepted the child. A moment later he led her into the waiting room. "A dog mauled her kitten," Will said, gently taking the scrap of gray fur from the little girl's hands. "Will you see what you can do while I take care of the owner?"

Alex took the kitten from him, her attention focused on a dangling and bloody front paw. She turned and rushed back to the operating room.

The kitten was lucky. The dog's teeth had broken its leg, but not damaged any vital organs. By the time the paw was set and bandaged Alex was already late for her appointment and the disgruntled owner of a Pekingese had departed, leaving a message on the counter to the effect that old Doctor Patterson never kept people waiting half an hour without a word of explanation.

Alex sighed. Old Doctor Patterson had had her—Alex —to make his excuses for him. She couldn't yet afford an assistant.

Will O'Keefe and the little girl, now happily licking an outsize ice cream cone, returned. "Her name is Consuela and the kitten is Ramon," Will said. "How is he?"

Alex smiled at the child. "Ramon will be just fine, Consuela, but I'd better keep him here overnight, just to be sure. Can you tell me what your address and phone number are?"

The little girl couldn't be any more than five years old.

She gave Alex a wary look, then shook her dark curls. "I mustn't tell anybody where I live."

"If it's your bill you're worried about . . ." Will began, his eyes narrowed in disdain. He pulled out a well-worn leather wallet.

Alex resisted the urge to kick his shin. She said, "Children sometimes bring in pets without telling their parents—and often they forget to pick them up." To Consuela she said, "All right, you have your Mommy or your Daddy call me and I'll let them know when Ramon can go home, okay?" She handed one of her business cards to the child, who took it and rushed outside, leaving a trail of dripping ice cream in her wake.

"How much do I owe you—for taking care of the kitten?" Will asked.

"The kitten has nothing to do with you. Apparently you think every veterinarian—and probably every physician—is more worried about getting paid than in healing the hurt and sick. Well, you're wrong, Mr. O'Keefe. Now will you please leave?"

His expression had softened somewhat. "Will, please call me Will. My late boss used to call me Mr. O'Keefe when he was angry with me. Tell me, whatever brought a nice girl like you to a place like Sand Point?"

"Are you inferring that Sand Point isn't a nice place? It's the loveliest little resort town on the southern California coast."

"Oh, I won't argue with you about the natural beauty of the area. But the town is owned lock, stock and barrel by the Barringtons. They decide who gets to live here, work here and even to vacation here. Not many people can afford the prices charged by the local innkeepers. This place is a mecca for the super-rich. There isn't a campground, or a low-priced motel for miles around. The Barringtons successfully kept freeways and rail lines well away from their private paradise."

"You're wrong about everyone here being rich. I'm not rich. I'm trying to pay off a mortgage; not that it's any of your business, but professional practices don't come cheap. And when you bring Meggie in tomorrow you'll meet Juan, who helps me out. His family isn't rich either."

"Juan? Ah, yes. He and his family live in the *barrio* on the other side of the hill, right? Carefully hidden from view. Since there's no railroad track they couldn't put them on the wrong side of the tracks, they simply live on the wrong side of the hill. The *Latino* workers who do all of the menial tasks and then vanish from view."

Alex allowed her eyes to flicker over his tattered clothes. "And what are *you* doing here, Will O'Keefe?"

"Fishing in the bay," he answered, his face a study of innocence.

"And what's your connection to the Barringtons?"

"Ah, so she told you about me."

"Not really. She said something about you being an unprincipled scoundrel."

He grinned. "That's the kindest thing a Barrington ever said about me."

"Where are you from? I've lived here for over a year and I've never heard your name mentioned before."

"I'm from here, there and everywhere. My connection, as you call it, to the Barringtons concerned some of Congressman Bart Barrington's activities in Sacramento."

A light suddenly dawned in the back of Alex's mind. "O'Keefe . . . now I remember. You're that reporter who accused Bart Barrington of catering to oil company interests. Something about offshore oil drilling and hints of bribes."

"Among other things."

"But . . . I thought your paper printed a retraction and you were fired from the newspaper."

"That's the story the Barringtons put out. Actually I quit to freelance when my editor-in-chief decided not to let me pursue the investigation."

"You're a fool to come to here. What do you possibly hope to gain? This is the Barrington's home. Nobody here is going to even talk to you, when they know who you are."

"I'm not here to continue the investigation into Bart's crooked politics. I no longer have a job as a reporter, remember?"

"What are you doing here then?"

"I told you," he explained patiently. "Fishing in the bay."

Just as she'd suspected. A sea-going drifter, without money, position, or even visible means of support. She shrugged. "I'm not really interested anyway."

Out of the corner of her eye she could see the two elderly ladies who owned her next patient climbing out of their Mercedes in front of the pet hospital.

Alex went to open the door for the Misses Munro, who were twin sisters with classic features and complexions like faded rose petals. They were followed by their chauffeur, carrying a large wrought-iron cage housing a brilliantly hued parrot named Ambrose. The spinster sisters had lived a chaste and exemplary life in a mansion left to them by their parents for as long as anyone could remember. Ambrose, however, had mysteriously appeared about six months ago, along with a mixed-breed female dog named Frances.

Neither parrot nor dog had come from the only pet store in town. Alex had inquired of the owner. The gaudy bird and scruffy dog seemed unlikely pets for the two genteel women, especially since Frances was forever digging her way out of the yard and running loose, and someone had taught Ambrose some very naughty words.

As Alex greeted the sisters Will said, "*Au revoir*. I'll see you tomorrow."

Ambrose cackled. "Take off your clothes, me beauty."

Rodney Barrington's gold Maserati glided to a halt in front of the pet hospital at five-thirty, just as Alex was locking up.

As usual, Rodney was immaculate in white slacks and a dark silk shirt. His black hair and thin mustache seemed to be enameled onto his head and upper lip, and one of the gold chains around his neck carried a tiny replica of a polo hat over crossed mallets.

He'd been away, in the South of France, when Alex first came to work for old Doctor Patterson. Rodney returned shortly after the old vet retired and Alex took over the practice. She'd been out with him a few times, but there was no spark to the relationship. She suspected that he really preferred the company of his polo ponies but liked being seen in the company of a beautiful woman. There wasn't much of substance behind his handsome exterior and his perfunctory good-night kiss hinted that his libido wasn't highly developed either. Alex had wondered at first if he were gay, but decided it was simply that he was asexual.

"Alex, my sweet, you look like a woman in need of a little pampering," Rodney announced, attempting to vault out of the sports car but stumbling awkwardly. He clutched the door for support and swore under his breath.

Alex hid a grin and wanted to point out that he really should learn to distinguish between a car and a horse. "Hello, Rodney."

"I thought a couple of stiff cocktails and then a quiet dinner . . ." Rodney began, opening the car door and gesturing for her to get in.

Typical of him not to call to inquire if she were free. "I'm sorry, I can't. I'm busy tonight." It was true, she had a stack of journals to read and later would have to come back to check on a sick spaniel.

He frowned. "This is the second time you've refused an invitation."

"Perhaps you should try calling me first," Alex suggested.

Rodney's gaze moved to a point over her shoulder, his mouth opening in surprise. Turning, she saw the formidable figure of Will O'Keefe, moving toward them with a boxer's grace. He'd changed into a fairly respectable pair of cords and a sports shirt, shaved, combed his hair. He must have been waiting in the coffee shop next door, which had several sidewalk tables, partially hidden by shrubs and vines. Will said, "Hi, Alex. Sorry I'm late."

He took her arm and slipped it through his. Alex had a sudden wild notion that she'd like to hug him, to feel herself enclosed by those powerful arms in a protective shield. Instead, she said, "Will O'Keefe . . . Rodney Barrington."

"*O'Keefe?*" Rodney repeated, taking an almost imperceptible step backward, his nostrils narrowing as though to ward off an odor.

Will smiled. *"Barrington,"* he said, with equal ardor. Then, turning to Alex said, "Shall we be on our way?"

Alex's five-year-old Ford was parked in front of the pet hospital, but she ignored it and strolled down the hill toward the setting sun on Will's arm. It seemed like a natural thing to do.

When they were out of Rodney's earshot, she said, "Why am I doing this? I didn't really need rescuing from him. I suppose you were waiting next door and over-heard our conversation?"

"Every word. I too was waiting for you with a dinner invitation."

"I told you this afternoon—"

"I caught more yellowtail than Meggie and I can eat. I thought we could build a fire on the beach. Nothing like fresh-caught fish sizzling over the coals, some crusty bread and a bottle of wine . . ."

"Yellowtail, huh?" Alex said, feeling suddenly raven-ous. "Are we going to walk to the beach, or shall we take my car?"

3

Alex lay on the still warm sand watching Will broil the fish steaks over coals glowing in a circle of rocks. Red Baron and Meggie were chasing the retreating tide and splashing each other playfully. On the horizon the sun sank in fiery splendor into a darkening sea. Will's boat, anchored beyond the offshore rocks, was a bobbing shadow.

Several thoughts swam through Alex's mind, vying for attention: Meggie should not bear a litter of Red Baron's puppies; Alex should not be fraternizing with an enemy of the Barringtons; Will O'Keefe was dangerously attractive—in a purely physical way, of course—and it was difficult for Alex to deal with other matters when the red-gold light of the fading sun tantalizingly bronzed his firm pectoral muscles and enormous shoulders. His biceps flexed slightly as he speared and turned the fish. She felt a small shiver ripple up her spine.

Upon arriving at the beach, he'd stripped off shirt and cords, revealing faded swim trunks. Alex had kicked off her shoes, but still wore the green cotton pants and surgical jacket she'd worked in. Her eyes, almost without conscious consent, kept slipping down the length of Will's body. A hunger that wasn't related to the appetizing smell of broiling fish was making itself felt somewhere deep inside her.

Clearing her throat, she said, "You're not really just here on vacation, are you?" The question surprised her because she thought she was going to bring up the subject of the dogs again.

He looked up, his eyes crinkling quizzically as his craggy face broke into a grin. "Writers never take vacations. The compulsion to write is always simmering on their back burners."

So he *was* here to harass the Barringtons. Alex let out her breath slowly, vowing silently that she would ignore this man's physical appeal and never see him again. She loved living in Sand Point and simply couldn't afford to befriend someone who was out to destroy the Barringtons, who, in turn, could easily destroy her.

Aloud, she said, "Why don't you forget the muckraking journalism and write a novel instead? Your hero could live on an ancient boat with his only companion—his faithful dog."

"Hey, now that's an idea. Everybody loves dog stories."

"You could call it *Man's Best Friend*."

"Well now, much as I love dogs in general and Meggie in particular, my own personal belief has always been that man's best friend is . ... woman."

Alex allowed herself to rise to the bait. "Oh? And is there a particular woman in your life?"

"I'm still searching for her. What about you? I can't believe you're serious about Rodney. *Is* there a serious contender?"

"You make it sound like a boxing match."

"The most promising male-female relationships are. A little initial hostility hones the perceptions to a fine edge. If you get the differences of opinion settled right away, then the scene is set for living happily ever after."

"An interesting theory."

"I expect to spar quite a bit with the woman I finally settle down with. We'll smooth out each other's rough edges and then grow old together in perfect harmony."

He was watching her with paralyzing intensity and Alex decided he was testing her in some way. She was tempted to respond that she personally didn't intend to even think about settling down for years yet. Instead, she murmured, "I hope you find a woman willing to spar with you. Most of the women I know would rather be gently romanced."

"Would you?" he asked immediately.

She thought about Rodney. Flowers delivered to the pet hospital occasionally, expensive chocolates sent to the cottage, several cards—Valentine, birthday, selected from the local card shop. In return, she was expected to be ready to spend an evening with him when he found time for her. Alex said brusquely, "I don't have time for such things at present. Not many men understand that there are times when a sick cat is more important than they are. And that reminds me, I've got to get back to look at a spaniel. How long before the fish is ready?"

"Just about done. How about getting the wine and bread out of the hamper?"

Alex lifted the lid and found a very good Chablis, along with a long loaf of French bread. There were even two wineglasses. "Hmm, a real class act," she commented. "I was expecting plastic."

He smiled. "Corkscrew wrapped in the napkins."

Red Baron, tiring of his game, came panting over to her and shook his auburn coat, sending a shower of salt water over her. Meggie followed, watching Red adoringly. Will said, "Down, you two." Both dogs flopped to the sand obediently.

"Very good," Alex said. "Exactly the right tone of command—tempered with love."

"Do you suppose it might work on a woman?"

"Not any more. We stopped being chattels, remember?" She took the paper plate he offered and sniffed appreciatively at the fish. Both dogs began to wag their tails.

Will served the two dogs their carefully filleted portions before coming to sit beside Alex. He picked up his glass and raised it. "To our grandchildren."

"What?" Alex almost dropped her plate.

He gestured toward the dogs. "We can't be sure yet, of course, but . . ."

"I refuse to drink to an accidental litter of pups. A responsible owner—" Alex began.

"Okay, okay, don't get testy. Let's wait and see, shall we? We don't even know Meggie is pregnant yet. Let's drink to a perfect sunset and the beginning of either a gentle romance or a lusty sparring match, how's that?"

"I'll drink to the sunset, but forget the rest." The aroma of the fish couldn't be ignored. Alex sipped the smooth wine and then fell upon the yellowtail in uninhibited delight. It was as delicious as it smelled. They demolished fish, bread and just about emptied the wine bottle before the long shadows of evening claimed the beach. The charcoal still glowed in the circle of rocks and the moon sailed out from behind the bluff.

Meggie had fallen asleep beside Red, their two bodies sleekly curved together, Meggie's head resting on Red's flank. Will slid closer to Alex and draped his arm across the rock behind her, not quite touching her, but close enough that her flesh felt his presence, even through the cotton material of her jacket.

"I really have to go and take care of the spaniel," Alex said, making a small circle in the sand with her fingertip. "Thank you for dinner. It was wonderful. Would you believe I've lived in the cottage for nearly a year and this is the first fresh fish from the bay I've eaten?"

"You're lucky to own the cottage. White-water view, your own beach, total privacy, yet close to town."

"Oh, it isn't mine. It belongs to—"

"The Barringtons. I should have guessed."

Reluctantly, Alex stood up. Will sprang to his feet also. "May I go with you?"

"No . . . no, I'd rather you didn't."

"Will you come back to the beach? I'll wait."

"Please don't. Look, Will . . . it would be better if we decide here and now what you want to do about Meggie and then go our separate ways."

His hand strayed toward hers, captured her fingers. Then his other hand went around her waist, pulling her gently but insistently closer to him. He leaned forward, bending his head toward her face and her chin tilted upward in some reflex action she hadn't anticipated.

Then his lips, tasting of the sea and all its mystery, were connected to hers.

What is it, she thought in surprise, about this kiss that makes it different from every other I've experienced? A slow, leisurely exploration of eager mouths, the feeling of wonder that a kiss could be so enthralling. Everything was exactly right. She liked the way Will felt, tasted; the tang of brine that clung to him was fresh and clean and impossibly seductive.

She wasn't sure how long they stood on the moonlit beach, kissing like it was a new discovery and theirs alone. Neither of them seemed inclined to draw apart. Then there was a slight whimper, and Red Baron's damp body wriggled between them.

Laughing, they broke away. "I think the green-eyed monster just reared its ugly head," Will said. "Shame on you, Red. I thought Meggie was your girl now."

"Why did you kiss me?" Alex asked.

"Originally, I think, to show you that two unsuitable creatures can be attracted to one another. Nature or sheer physical chemistry, or something, doesn't care about pedigrees. Red and Meggie. You and me."

"So you think we're different breeds too, do you?"

"The refined lady veterinarian catering to the pampered pets of the super-rich and the cashiered journalist of dubious repute. Yes, I'd say that society would frown on our friendship, never mind anything else between us. But that doesn't stop us from finding each other . . . attractive, does it?"

"The spaniel . . ." Alex muttered weakly, and turned and ran back up the beach on wobbly legs.

He called after her, "Turn on your back porch light

when you get back if you want some company. I can see it from the boat."

The telephone's shrill ring jolted Alex from a fretful sleep. A gray dawn was breaking over a leaden sea. As she reached for the receiver her first memory was of how close she'd come to turning on her porch light last night, even though it was after midnight when she got home. It was ridiculous how appealing she found Will O'Keefe. She had to nip those feelings in the bud.

"Hello? This is Alex Aimes."

"Alex . . . Mrs. Barrington. You must come to the house right away. Star coughed this morning. I'm afraid he must have picked up some germs in your office yesterday."

"It would be a little early for a virus to develop, Mrs. Barrington—and he wasn't in contact with any other animal. But, of course, I'll come if you think he's sick."

The telephone clicked in her ear. Her alarm hadn't gone off yet. It was barely five-thirty. She went into the bathroom and turned on the shower, peered at herself in the mirror. Her eyes were heavy with sleep, but there was something new about her face. She wasn't sure what it was. A certain eagerness to see what the day would bring, perhaps, despite it's unpromising start.

She showered briefly, then twisted her shoulder-length hair up into a tawny topknot. She'd considered having it cut short, but her hairdresser had warned her that if she cropped her hair she'd probably have to present her ID wherever she went.

It was true, there was a fragile quality to her features that suggested untried youth, despite the fact that she was almost twenty-eight. Longer hair did add sophistication, especially when she put it up. In her profession people seemed to expect muscular men capable of wrestling Great Danes to the floor. She'd lost several clients who shared this feeling and who now drove to the next town with their pets, despite the fact that the former Sand Point veterinarian had been a frail old man. Dr. Patterson had hired husky young high school boys to place themselves between the animal's teeth and their veterinarian.

Grabbing an orange to eat en route, Alex hurried out to her car, which she'd left parked on the driveway last night. She glanced in the direction of Will's boat, wondering if he were up yet, and what he'd be doing today. Damn, she had to forget the man; he was too much of a complication in her life right now.

Her ailing Ford protested noisily as she coaxed it up the steep hills toward the Barrington's estate. A misty rain fell and Alex knew that after the driest winter on record she ought to be glad of the needed moisture, but if it developed into a real storm, what about that boat anchored in the bay?

There I go again, she warned herself as she reached the electronically-controlled gates of the Barrington's walled six-million-dollar estate. What do I care if his boat is smashed on the rocks?

"Dr. Aimes," she told the intercom. The gates slid open.

A brick driveway wound through rolling lawns and shimmering fountains, past a private nine-hole golf course, ending in front of a blindingly-white stucco building that anyone would have been proud to call home, but was actually a ten-car garage, over which were servants quarters.

The main house was built on the highest point of the twenty-acre estate. The family reached the house by means of an elevator from the garages to a breeze-way connected to the upper terrace.

Leaving her car in front of the garages, Alex walked up marble steps to a lower terrace which led to the tradesmen's entrance. She had never been invited to use the front doors.

A young man with sun-streaked hair and a surfer's tan, wearing a dark suit and white shirt, responded to the doorbell. Alex had never seen him before. "I'm Dr. Aimes, the veterinarian," she said. "I don't believe we've met?"

He opened the door wider, giving her a slightly insolent leer. "Come in, she's expecting you. Oh, yeah, I'm Marvin, the new butler."

Alex managed to keep her surprise to herself. A more unlikely-looking butler she'd never seen. Still, the old one had been even more ancient than the chauffeur, so she supposed he had been due to retire. She walked into the huge kitchen beyond the tradesmen's door, where several *Latina* maids were at work. They turned and regarded Marvin with flashing dark eyes as he passed by.

He led Alex to the solarium, running the length of the rear of the house and affording a perfect view of the ocean, from dark horizon to white surf breaking on pale sandy shore. The town of Sand Point curled around the bay like a beached shrimp, all pink and white stucco interspersed with red tile. Every house and cottage straight from the pages of *Beautiful Homes and Gardens*. Poverty didn't exist here, Will was right about that.

Mrs. Barrington sat on a white wicker couch, Star of

the East beside her, his head on her lap. A coffee pot and croissants waited on a glass-topped table.

"Good morning, Mrs. Barrington." Alex unzipped her medical bag and bent over the dog, who certainly didn't look sick. She supposed she'd better take his temperature, to satisfy his overanxious owner.

"Alex, dear, I want you to start calling me Amelia. And do have some coffee and croissants before you look at Star."

Almost dropping her bag in surprise, Alex said, "Oh . . . thank you . . . Amelia."

Marvin filled two fragile china cups with coffee, used silver tongs to transfer croissants to gold-rimmed plates and stood waiting for further commands. Alex sat down on the wicker couch.

"Thank you, Marvin, that will be all." Amelia turned to Alex as the butler departed and added in a stage whisper, "He should be addressed by his surname, of course, but we can't pronounce it." She laughed and Alex squirmed, since Marvin must have heard what she said.

"Now, my dear, there are a couple of things I'd like to discuss with you." Amelia's tone became businesslike. "First, I was awakened very early by Star coughing. If he caught a cold, then he must have got it at your office, so in future I shall need you to make house calls."

Alex said stiffly, "I can certainly do that, of course, but if he's having any respiratory problems it's possible that he's spending too much time indoors in a heated house. He really needs fresh air and exercise."

Ignoring the comment, Amelia went on, "Secondly, I want you to come to a little party I'm giving next Saturday. A charity affair. I want to raise money to gather enough signatures for a petition to outlaw the backyard breeding of dogs." She paused, as though expecting a round of applause, then added almost as an afterthought, "Oh, yes, and to build a shelter to house stray pets, so they don't have to be destroyed at the pound."

Combine a worthy cause with one of dubious value, Alex thought, and what do we have? But who could refuse to support the building of a pet haven? She swallowed some coffee and said, "Thank you, I'm free on Saturday. What time?"

"About seven, formal dress. And Rodney will be your escort, of course. Now, now, no need to get coy with me. I know my son is interested in you."

Alex couldn't think of a response, so began her examination of the Shar-pei. As she'd suspected, he was the picture of health. Probably had coughed to clear his throat. She would leave some vitamin C tablets and a small quantity of cough medicine, that should satisfy Amelia.

Amelia Barrington watched her every move, then suddenly pounced. "Now, there's one more thing I want to discuss with you. Rodney tells me that last night you had an assignation with that dreadful man O'Keefe."

"An assignation?" Alex heard the edge in her voice.

"You declined my son's invitation in order to accompany the man, didn't you?"

Lord, Alex thought, save me from a Momma's boy. "What is it you want to say to me, Amelia? You're surely not going to tell me I can't associate with whomever I choose?"

"When it comes to O'Keefe, that's exactly what I'm going to tell you. I'm sorry, Alex, but if you're seen with that man again, then there is no longer a place for you in Sand Point."

4

Will and Meggie were on the beach when Alex finished her long working day. That afternoon Alex had checked Meggie, found her to be in very good health, taken care of her flea problem and lectured Will on the proper grooming of his dog.

Now as Will tossed a stick of driftwood and Meggie chased it, then teased him with it, Alex saw that Meggie was back to her disheveled state. Will wore swim trunks and, even from the cottage window, Alex could see that the trunks and his hair were wet, as was Meggie's golden coat. They'd no doubt recently enjoyed a swim. Red Baron watched them forlornly as he paced up and down his chain-link fenced dog run.

The rain had been only a light shower and in the late afternoon the sun had broken through the cloud cover. Alex slipped out of her working clothes, donned khaki shorts and a shirt, and went out onto the back porch, which led to the dog run. Red Baron greeted her with his usual enthusiasm.

Down on the beach Will looked up and waved.

Alex opened the gate and Red rushed happily down the rough steps cut into the cliff. Picking up a teeth-marked rubber ball, Alex followed. Just because O'Keefe had decided to use the beach, there was no reason to forego her daily habit of playing with Red on the sand, which helped her unwind.

Will was waiting for her at the foot of the cliff when she reached the last step. The two dogs, side by side, galloped toward the tide pools.

"'Evening, Alex," Will said, his welcoming smile lighting up the beach, "You look mighty fetching tonight. How's the sick spaniel?"

"Much better."

"And Ramon?"

"He's fine too. But Consuela didn't come back and I haven't heard from her parents." She began to jog along the beach after the dogs.

Will fell into step beside her. "I'm sorry; you did say there'd be that possibility. I suppose it's possible her parents are illegals? They'd be afraid you'd notify the border patrol."

"Juan will keep an eye out for Consuela and return her kitten to her." Alex tried to quicken her pace, but he kept up easily and wasn't even breathing heavily.

Eventually, thoroughly winded, Alex stopped and collapsed to the sand. Will dropped down beside her. He reached out and gently pushed a loose strand of her hair back from her brow. There was something so infinitely caring about the gesture that Alex inexplicably felt a tear sting the back of her eye. It had been a long time since anyone took care of even the slightest of her needs.

"Do you always drive yourself so hard?" Will asked gently.

She struggled to catch her breath. "I'm a little out of condition, that's all."

"I didn't mean only the jogging. I know a little about the torturous task of getting through medical school. The attrition rate for vets is even higher than that for doctors, isn't it? You're pretty young to be in practice. It's taken a lot of dedication and sacrifice, I'm sure. And I noticed this afternoon how hard you work."

"I'm older than I look," Alex muttered. He was the first person she'd met who had even considered what she might have endured to get where she was today and his recognition of her struggle and accomplishment was more endearing than he could know.

"We—Meggie and I—caught red snapper today."

"Oh, no . . ." Alex began, thinking uncomfortably of Amelia Barrington's warning not to associate with him.

His smile faded. "I suppose fish two days in a row isn't too great an idea."

"It isn't that," Alex went on feeling thoroughly ashamed of her fleeting wisp of cowardice. "It's just that I picked up some Italian sausage on the way home and I thought I'd have spaghetti."

"Great!" Will said, mistaking the information for an invitation. "I can put the snapper in the ice box."

Since there was no way she could graciously forestall his coming to dinner, half an hour later they were sipping Burgundy in her kitchen while the pasta cooked. The two dogs, sated with dog food, were contentedly snoozing under the table.

"I picked up a copy of the *Bulletin* today," Will remarked. "It's a coincidence that Amelia is mounting a campaign to outlaw all but kennel breeding, isn't it?"

Alex glanced at him sharply. "You don't think it had anything to do with Red and Meggie do you? Mrs. Barrington has always been very active in various animal charities and so on. If any one incident sparked this current idea of hers, it was probably the Misses Munro suddenly acquiring Frances. They were the two maiden ladies who brought the parrot in while you were at the pet hospital."

"Frances is the parrot?"

"No, that's Ambrose. They acquired a mixed-breed female dog named Frances at the same time. Very mysterious. Nobody knows where the two animals came from. And the Misses Munro aren't talking. My own hunch is that they're taking care of them for a friend. Frances is forever escaping from their yard and she hasn't been spayed, but the old ladies said they hadn't been given permission for the operation."

"You're having a helluva time sterilizing the dogs in this town, aren't you?" Will asked with a wry grin.

"I am in favor of putting a stop to the appalling numbers of unwanted animals that are born, but for your information, my first concern is the health of the animals." She got up and went to the stove in response to the buzzer indicating that the spaghetti was done.

"Tell me about the Misses Munro. I love a mystery."

"Nothing much to tell. Old money . . . they live in a mansion on the hill overlooking the marina. They inherited everything when their parents were lost with all hands and their yacht somewhere off the southern tip of the Baja peninsula. Rumor has it that one of the sisters,

I'm not sure which, had a tragic love affair, years ago when she was young."

"They looked as alike as the proverbial two peas in the pod."

"No wonder, they're identical twins." She poured the sauce over the pasta, arranged the sausage around the edge of the dish and carried it to the table. "You're not thinking of really writing a novel about this town, are you? I mean, I'd hate to embarrass two nice old ladies."

Will laughed. "No, no novel. Just my journalist's over-developed curiosity about people. The pasta smells wonderful, by the way."

Alex took the Parmesan and gestured for him to help himself. "Isn't freelancing a rather precarious existence?"

He nodded, spooning pasta onto his plate. "That it is."

"Then why don't you go back to work on a newspaper or magazine?"

"I've tried both, but I like the freedom of writing to please myself, even if it isn't as financially rewarding."

"Your present lifestyle does mean that you can pull up stakes easily—or anchors, I suppose I should say, and move on. I've always been suspicious of men who can't put down roots."

"Some men have places to go and things to do before they settle down. I'm one of them. Better to do it now rather than wait until after I've married a woman and started a family, like some men."

There was no way he could have known that Alex's father had deserted them while she was still a child, nor could he have been aware of the poverty she and her mother had endured. Alex had been careful to erase all traces of that hungry, barefoot child from the educated woman she now was. She said, "Listen, right after we've eaten, I'm afraid I'm going to have to ask you to leave. And I really would appreciate it if you'd anchor your boat off some other beach."

His dark eyes regarded her with an uncomfortably knowing gaze, but he made no comment.

After a moment Alex added defensively, "Well, the Barringtons do own this cottage and I can't afford the rent on anything else in town. If they kick me out I'll either have to sleep in one of the cages, or have a long drive down the coast." She paused, waiting for him to comment, but although he had listened intently, he was now devoting all of his attention to the spaghetti.

"Well?" Alex asked at length.

"Well, what?"

"Will you move your boat?"

"If you insist."

Feeling somewhat deflated, Alex picked up her fork. The silence between them was not a companionable one. She sensed an inner turbulence in him that made her uneasy. Unable to stand it any longer, she burst out, "All right! Mrs. Barrington threatened to put me out of business if I associated with you."

Instantly he put his fork down, stood up and came around to her side of the table. Taking her hands, he drew her to her feet and wrapped her in a bear hug. She nestled against his chest gratefully, thinking of all the hugs she'd missed since coming to Sand Point. Will said, "Nobody has the right to choose your friends for you, you know. Ask yourself what's the worst she can do?"

"Oh, nothing much—kick me out of the cottage and the pet hospital, since both are owned by a Barrington real estate company. Then there's my loan at the bank, the one I took out to buy the old vet's practice, I guess they could foreclose on that."

"You have a lease on the cottage and the pet hospital?"

Alex nodded.

"Okay, so long as you pay your rent on both places, they can't kick you out. Nor can they foreclose on your loan so long as you're making payments. Alex . . ." He placed a finger under her chin and tipped her face. "Look at me. Now, tell me honestly that you don't want to see me again."

She sighed. "Why did you have to come along right now? Everything was going so well."

"Sure it was. You'd have toed the line, mixed with the right people, bought all the right brands. Rodney would have courted you in a halfhearted way and probably, since you're the prettiest woman in town and he's the local catch, you'd have married him. After that he'd have talked you into sharing your practice with a couple of partners, so all you'd get to do would be to treat ailing goldfish. Eventually you'd give up practising altogether to have two point four children and spend your days planning charity fundraisers, like Amelia. Come on, Alex, do you really think that kind of life would make you happy?"

She pulled free angrily, grabbed their plates and clattered them into the sink. "There's nothing wrong in wanting an orderly life. Look, I'm not a rebel, I admit it. I don't like discord. I don't *want* to rock the boat here. I love living and practising here and I worked damned hard to get what I have. Yes, I do want some of the comforts and finer things of life. And, since you ask, yes, I can honestly say that I don't want to see you again. You're just not my sort of . . . friend. You're a drifter, a beach-bum, a rabble-rouser who can't hold a job. Tell me, have you ever finished anything you started?"

Turning to collect the rest of the dishes, she collided with him. His arms went around her again and he said softly, "I'd like to finish making love to you . . . I dreamed about that kiss on the beach all night long."

Taken by surprise, she didn't move her head in time and in the instant his lips grazed hers, she knew she'd made the fatal mistake of responding to the urgency of the physical attraction that simmered between them like a volcano.

She closed her eyes, as if to make him vanish from sight, but surrendered her mouth to his. His hands caressed her back, slid to her waist and slipped under her shirt to find the warm flesh beneath.

The touch of his fingertips sent a shock wave radiating upward and she felt her nipples grow poised, expectant. She resisted the urge to grab his hand and guide it to her breast, flinging her head backward to end the kiss. "Let go of me. I . . . don't want this."

His hands fell to his sides instantly. "*This?* Or me? All right, Alex. I'll go. Come on, Meggie, let's not overstay our welcome."

Every primal instinct in her body shrieked for him to stay, to take her in his arms again and make love to her with all the passion she'd felt in his touch. She clamped her lips together as if to stop the words from escaping without her permission.

At the door he turned and looked back at her over his

shoulder. "If you change your mind don't forget, I can see your porch light from my boat. I'll keep my present anchorage for one more night—just in case."

She stood at the sink for several minutes after the door closed behind him. Then rushed outside and with trembling fingers removed the light bulb from the wrought-iron lantern attached to the back porch.

5

~~∞∞∞∞∞∞∞∞∞∞∞~~

Juan Gonzales was finishing cleaning the outdoor pens when Alex arrived. A slender, wiry youth with smooth olive-skin and sad amber eyes, he helped support a widowed mother and two younger sisters, and in addition to working for Alex, also worked the late shift at one of the gas stations in town.

"*Buenos dias, señorita,*" he said. "I found the child, Consuela, and her mother. But the kitten didn't really belong to Consuela. Her mother said it was a stray."

"If she'll let the child have the kitten, tell the mother it will grow into a healthy cat and there's no charge for setting the paw."

Juan's face broke into a smile. "*Sí, señorita.* You are a very kind person. Oh, I almost forgot. Miss Munro called. She said Frances had dug under the fence again. I said I'd try to find her."

"You'd better leave now then, and don't be late for school, okay?"

Alex dragged herself through her morning appointments, feeling let-down, disappointed, cheated in some way, yet unwilling to admit the source of her discontent. Remembering a psychology course she'd taken once, she slipped a rubber band on her wrist and snapped it every time Will O'Keefe popped into her mind. It didn't help much and after a while, feeling foolish, she took it off.

At noon, with all of her chores caught up during her frenzied morning rush, she decided to walk down to the marina and lunch on fish tacos from a vendor who had recently set up a stand where the incoming fishermen berthed. He cooked the fish over a hibachi, wrapped it in warm tortillas and offered a variety of toppings to complete the taco. Since it was only a matter of time until the outraged restauranteurs of the town ran him off, Alex was looking forward to at least one more lunch from his stand.

The day was sunlit and sparklingly clear. Spring was at its zenith and no doubt that was the reason a young woman's fancy had lightly turned to thoughts of . . . not love, perhaps, but certainly a healthy lust. Take your bronzed muscles and get out of my mind, Will O'Keefe.

Her copy of the *Bulletin* still lay on the sidewalk in front of the pet hospital, so she picked it up and took it with her. The front page was devoted to Amelia Barrington's forthcoming charity ball. *Ball?* Alex tucked the newspaper under her arm and considered the state of her wardrobe. There was nothing in it even remotely resembling a ball gown.

Where the main street met the sea, rows of yachts and sailboats were neatly lined up in the marina, their masts like exclamation points against a cloudless sky. Alex walked past the marina and pier to the sandy beach where the fishermen dragged their boats ashore, their catches still squirming in the nets.

The taco stand was under the pier, partially hidden from the street by the boats on the beach. She kicked off her shoes to walk on the soft dry sand, wondering if Will had sailed his boat out of sight of her cove by now.

As she negotiated the clutter of boats, a black and tan dog darted across her path.

"Frances!" Alex dived for her, but missed. She chased the dog around the boats, as some of the fishermen attempted unsuccessfully to intercept the bounding animal.

Frances had become cunning in the ways of the chase, and after a minute or two disappeared from view. Breathless, Alex gave up and headed for the taco stand.

The owner of the stand was a weather-beaten old man with the faded blue eyes of the seaman. Today there was no appetizing smell of cooking fish and warm tortillas. He was packing his hibachi into a cardboard box, next to one already filled with his condiments.

He looked up as Alex approached, and spread his hands regretfully. "Sorry, no lunch today. They closed me down. Hell, you shoulda seen the posse they sent! Health department, business license manager—even a border patrol agent. Reckon they figured I must be Mexican 'cause I was fixin' tacos."

Disappointed, Alex sat down on one of his boxes. "That's too bad. What will you do now?"

"Move on. Try to find another spot."

"Those fish tacos were awfully good. Why don't you see if you can get a job at one of the local restaurants?"

He regarded her with amazement, his wizened features breaking into a gargoyle grin. "You've gotta be kidding! Who'd hire an old geezer like me? 'Sides, I wouldn't like to be cooped up in no kitchen all day."

"Couldn't you apply for a business license then? Set up your stand legally?"

He scratched his thinning gray hair. "They'd want stuff like an address and what I've been up to these past thirty, forty years, right?"

Alex hid a smile. "What *have* you been up to?"

"Merchant marine. Sailed all over the world until I got in a bit of trouble in the China Sea and lost my ticket—third engineer's ticket, that is. After that I mostly bummed around."

Alex knew there was little hope that the rigidly run city government of Sand Point would permit a disreputable-looking old sea dog to move in on their super-homogenized merchants, but she lingered, trying to think of a way to help him. He told her his name was Cosmo and she introduced herself and helped him carry his boxes to a rusting Chevy parked illegally beside the pier and already ticketed by an alert meter maid.

On their last trip to collect his belongings, a black and tan dog came skulking around the pier supports, eyes fixed on Cosmo.

In the split second that it took for Alex to react and grab the dog, it occurred to her that Frances probably had been given a handout by Cosmo and no doubt had also become addicted to fish tacos.

Frances was most likely part shepherd and part collie, a large, strongly-muscled animal. Alex lost her balance and rolled on the sand, still clutching the dog's collar. Frances began to bark excitedly and Alex feared she was losing ground, when all at once a leathery old hand tapped the dog's muzzle and Cosmo yelled, "Hit the deck!"

The dog's barking became an ingratiating whine and she flopped down on the sand and turned belly up, tail thumping the ground furiously. Alex looked up at the old man in amazement as he slipped a length of rope through the dog's collar. "Wow, Cosmo. I've heard of animal magnetism, but . . ."

"Pesky mutt. I fed her some fish yesterday. Shoulda knowed better."

Alex scrambled to her feet, dusting sand from her slacks, and Cosmo handed her the end of the rope. "You take her home, Doc. If I show up at somebody's door, they'll call out the cavalry for sure."

Frances was rubbing herself against the old man's leg, licking his boots.

"Cosmo, wait," Alex said impulsively as he turned to leave. She had to help him in some way, but she doubted he'd take a job as a vet's helper, even if she hadn't already hired Juan. She could offer him some money, perhaps? Would he accept it?

Before she had a chance to say anything, Cosmo said, "Don't you fret none about me, little lady. I shoulda knowed I wouldn't get away with setting up in Sand Point. Just couldn't resist trying though. But I'll be jes' fine. I've got a place to go."

He got into the Chevy and turned the key in the

ignition. Frances tugged wildly at the rope until Alex caught sight of a passing taxi and hailed it. She told the driver, "Take me to the Munro mansion, please."

Fifteen minutes later one of the Munro sisters—Alex could never tell them apart—thanked her and scolded Frances. In the background Ambrose the parrot joyfully screamed a choice four-letter word at the return of the prodigal.

Returning to the pet hospital, Alex was confronted by the spectacle of Will and Meggie getting busted. A patrol car was parked at the curb and the officer was writing a ticket as Will leaned unconcernedly against a lamppost. Meggie sat quietly at his feet, her expression more guilt-ridden than her owner's. "Hi, Alex," Will said.

"What's going on?" Alex asked.

The young officer said, "No leash," and finished writing the citation. Will signed it, received his copy and the patrol car went on its way.

Alex shook her head in disbelief. "They usually only give a warning, the first time. I should have told you there's a strict leash law in town."

"Oh, I knew it," Will answered. "It's just that Meggie doesn't usually need one. She'll walk to heel if I ask her nicely. Watch this."

He held out his hand, as though holding the end of a leash, then said, "Come, Meggie." She trotted beside him, never varying the distance between them, as though she really were on an invisible leash. Alex grinned, in spite of herself.

"Come on inside. I'll get you a real leash. Keep you both out of trouble."

Inside the waiting room, Alex added casually, "Why don't you give me that ticket too? I'll take care of it."

"No thanks. I pay my own fines. Besides, I don't want you involved. I know the word has probably gone out to make my stay in town as uncomfortable as possible. In fact, I just dropped in to tell you that I did change my anchorage, but I intend to sail past your cove every night at sunset . . . just in case your porch light is ever left on."

Alex dangled a leather leash in one hand and a chain in the other. "Which would you prefer?"

He selected the leather one and their fingers touched briefly. Alex was afraid if she looked into his eyes he'd see that a small shock wave had passed up her arm and registered in that part of her mind reserved for sensory images. Will was dressed in jeans and shirt, but he might as well have been stripped to the waist, because Alex was acutely aware of the muscles beneath the shirt and remembered the way his arms felt when they encircled her.

"I doubt my porch light will be left on," she said in a strangely husky tone.

He bent to attach the leash to Meggie's collar. "You going to Amelia's fundraiser on Saturday?"

She cleared her throat. "I've been invited. Yes, I suppose so. I imagine everyone in town will be there."

"The *Bulletin* says that tickets are available at a hundred bucks a throw."

Alex hadn't been aware of that, but since Amelia had made it clear Alex was to be both an invited guest and Rodney's dinner date, she hoped there was no need to worry about the donation, which would cripple her budget.

"How much do I owe you?" Will asked.

She drew a blank, until he waved the end of the leash. "Oh, that. No charge."

He shook his head slightly, then pulled out his wallet and deposited a ten-dollar bill on the counter. "Good-bye, Alex. Don't forget about the porch light. Come on, Meggie. I'll spring you from the chain gang as soon as the yard bulls are out of sight."

"That's too much . . ." Alex called after him, picking up the ten dollars. But he and Meggie were already sauntering down the street.

That evening at sunset Alex stood behind the bougainvillea-covered trellis on her back porch and watched a sailboat glide slowly around the bay.

It was Will's boat, of course. Even if she hadn't recognized the shape of the sloop, she could see the silhouette of Meggie sitting on the bow, gazing at the shoreline and no doubt longing for Red Baron almost as much as Alex longed for Will O'Keefe.

Red whined and paced the redwood porch restlessly, equally lonely for his lady love. "Dammit, Red," Alex said, "we were perfectly happy before they came along. We can be again."

He gave her a reproachful glance and flopped down, his head on his paws in defeat.

"They're totally unsuitable for us. Not our kind of people at all," Alex told him sternly. "Like it or not, there are class boundaries we all have to observe. It doesn't really have anything to do with discrimination; it has to do with acceptance by our peers. The garbage collector wouldn't really be happy living in the palace with the queen and the charwoman wouldn't know how to deal with the lifestyle of the senator. We all have our place in the scheme of things and we're more comfortable with people of our own background and education. Now, Will O'Keefe, for instance, he's most likely from the kind of background I had to fight to escape—and I don't want to go back to it.''

Red Baron closed his eyes, as though in disbelief.

"I am *not* a snob," Alex said. "Oh, you! You're just a big mass of instincts. I understand those primal urges of yours very well but I can't indulge in them with Will. Once the passion died, what would we do together? Can you see me bumming around on a boat? He's some kind of seagoing hippie and I'm a successful professional woman. Why, he doesn't even own a decent set of clothes. I'd never get to eat in a nice restaurant again . . ." She paused, aghast. "God, is this me saying this? Well, nevertheless, we have to let them go. Believe me, it's better this way."

The sun had sunk below the horizon and the brief southern twilight was already fading. Running lights came on as Will's boat headed for the open sea.

Aboard the sloop, Will hung the lantern from the bulkhead, then scooped dog food from a can into Meggie's dish with one hand, his other on the rudder.

"You might just as well come and eat. We're not going ashore," he told her.

Meggie continued to sit on the bow, staring at the dark outline of the land. She whined plaintively as she realized they were cresting the long swells of the open sea and the shoreline was growing more distant.

Will set a course for an isolated cove further along the coast and after a moment Meggie came and sat beside him, ignoring the dish of food.

He rubbed her ear, and fondled the thick fur of her

neck. "I know, girl, it hurts like hell, doesn't it? But we're not wanted and why should we be? It's not that they don't like us. It's just that we're a complication they can do without right now."

Later, after he'd dropped anchor and chewed disinterestedly on a peanut butter sandwich, he placed a portable typewriter on the small table in the cabin, and inserted a blank sheet of paper.

He typed: TO HAVE OR HAVE NOT, *A question of affordable housing. While the California State Legislature is deciding whether to rule that all suburbs are required by the state Constitution to permit construction of inexpensive housing, exclusionary zoning in the beach resort of Sand Point not only keeps out the poor, but also denies access to middle-income families."*

Frowning, he x'd out *access* and typed *housing* above it. Then crossed out his heading and replaced it with, HAVENS FOR THE SUPER-RICH.

Then he pulled the sheet of paper from the typewriter and tossed it into a plastic trash bag hanging from the bulkhead. He stared at the bare typewriter platen, seeing Alex's face, remembering how his hand felt on her waist, recalling the yielding sweetness of her mouth and his own surging desire when he kissed her. He blinked away her image and reached for another sheet of paper.

In this town, he wrote, *the leading citizens not only want to bar from residence everyone who isn't wealthy, but have mounted a campaign to eliminate even pets who aren't bluebloods. Funds are being raised to introduce legislation that would ban all but kennel breeding—*

He broke off, thinking of Alex again. The article in the *Bulletin* had stated that the Sand Point veterinarian, Dr.

Alex Aimes, would accompany Rodney Barrington to his mother's fund-raising ball.

Yanking the page from his typewriter again, Will crumpled it into a ball. But this time a slow smile was spreading across his face. Nothing like a plan of action to lift the gloom. Yes! He was going to do it . . .

6

~∞∞∞∞∞∞∞∞∞~

Alex stared at the dress box, tissue paper and pale pink satin spilling over the sides. Trembling with anger, she ripped open the accompanying note. It was from Amelia Barrington.

"My dear . . . please wear this gown tonight. It's a designer original. I do so want you to make a good impression on our friends and, of course, there will be media representatives present."

Alex looked up at the messenger who had delivered the box and who waited expectantly. The logo on the box indicated the dress had come from the most exclusive boutique in town. Alex said, "Wait a minute." She went into the bedroom, fished a five-dollar bill out of her purse and went back to the cottage door.

"Take it back. I'm refusing it. Here, this is for your trouble."

Crumpling Amelia's note in her hand as she went, Alex

strode back into the bedroom. The nerve of the woman! The utter gall! Alex considered calling Amelia and telling her she wasn't going to the fundraising ball tonight, but Rodney had telephoned and in a touchingly uncharacter-istic display of humility, expressed his pleasure that Alex would be his date.

Since tonight's affair was a command performance for every family in town, it would be difficult for Rodney to find a substitute date at such short notice. Besides, he couldn't help having a battle-ax for a mother. A small inner voice suggested that perhaps he could help being such a wimp, but Alex decided to ignore it.

Laid out on her bed were the only possibilities to wear tonight. A three-year-old cocktail dress of blue chiffon that had been ruined at a graduation party when an exuberant new Ph.D had spilled wine all over the skirt, and a jumpsuit she'd picked up in a thrift store with the idea of taking it apart and making a blouse from the garnet red silk. The jumpsuit was far too Fredericks of Hollywood in style for her taste, but now, remembering that ghastly pink satin gown Amelia had wanted her to wear, Alex slipped out of her jeans and into the jumpsuit.

The top was cut in an ingenious way that presented a fairly high neckline in front, but was slashed to the waist in back, clinging precariously to the very edges of her shoulders. There was no way a bra could be worn with it, which meant the thin silk, although of a dense enough color to be opaque, would certainly clearly reveal the shape of her nipples. The pants were a little long, but would be fine if she wore very high heels. She had one pair, left over from her early college disco days.

Still smarting from Amelia's patronizing gesture, Alex rummaged in her closet for the evening sandals. Rhinestone trimmed, strappy, four-and-a-half-inch heels. She held them in her hands for a moment wondering where that carefree girl had gone. Was she still there, buried under layer upon layer of conservative, work-dedicated professionalism? The only clothes she'd bought since coming to Sand Point had been a rather matronly suit and sensible blouse. A dress-for-success outfit, dictated by some male, somewhere, who'd written that the only way women could compete in the business and professional world was by mimicking masculine attire, along with their mores.

A moment later she stood in front of her dresser and unfastened her hair, shook it loose and ran her fingers through it until it turned into a wild palomino blonde mane. Yes, she thought. Out of control. That's the look I want for tonight. Thanks, Amelia, for sending over that blasted dress. It was just what I needed to jolt me into getting back onto my hind legs. Now, blue eye shadow to set off the blue eyes, and a strong lipstick, no mere hint of glosser and subtle mascara for tonight, oh, no . . .

Rodney blinked several times in rapid succession when Alex opened the cottage door. "Alex?" It was more of a question than a statement, as though he wasn't sure who was facing him. He wore a black tuxedo and carried a plastic-boxed white orchid.

"Come in, Rodney, I just have to feed Red before we go. This for me? Thank you." She took the orchid from him and, since there was no way it could be pinned to the delicate silk of the jumpsuit, put it in her hair.

Rodney followed her in hushed silence as she went into the kitchen to finish preparing Red's dinner. As a special treat, since the setter would be left alone all evening, she was chopping liver for him.

"Ugh!" Rodney exclaimed. "How can you handle raw liver? I'll wait for you in the living room. You . . . uh . . . look very nice, Alex. That outfit is . . . uh . . . quite a change from what you usually wear."

Alex mixed the liver into the dry dog food in Red's dish and couldn't help wishing it were Will O'Keefe who was escorting her tonight. At his side she'd face Amelia and the stuffy old guard of Sand Point with all of the reckless bravado she'd felt when she dressed in this crazy sexy outfit. But accompanied by a black tuxedo . . .

As the gold Maserati bore her toward the Barringtons' estate, Alex found herself thinking that probably part of Will's attraction for her was his utter disregard of material things, along with an unabashed lack of pedigree. At the same time, these were traits she couldn't accept in a man because she'd carefully eliminated them from her own image, years ago. Certain adjustments—compromises— were necessary in order to achieve professional status.

The grounds of the Barrington estate were ablaze with light, playing on fountains, softly gilding marble statuary, spotlighting shrubbery and gleaming on the forest of Rolls-Royces, Mercedes and Cadillacs that said a good number of guests had already arrived.

As they rode the elevator up to the main floor of the house, Alex felt some of her new-found courage evaporate. She wondered if she could affect a faint, claim sudden illness and have Rodney take her home. He was staring in apparent stupification at the outline of her breasts under the red silk. Perhaps he wasn't asexual after all.

Before she realized it, the elevator doors opened and she was in a huge drawing room under a dazzling array of chandeliers, surrounded by women wearing Dior and Givenchy gowns, dripping diamonds. Their men wore black tuxedos, like so many penguins. White-coated servants carrying trays of champagne glasses and hors d'oeuvres moved ghostlike among the guests.

Alex grabbed a glass and drained it before the servant could move on, replaced the empty glass on his tray and picked up another. Rodney watched in astonishment.

Congressman Bart Barrington, a short balding man with a permanent affable smile and eyes that never rested long in one place, was in center stage. He always seemed to be filibustering. But it was Amelia Barrington who caught Alex's petrified attention.

Amelia, resplendent in a white satin gown, bore down on them like an angel of wrath. Her eyes glittered more fiercely than her diamonds, as they took in every detail of Alex's jumpsuit, but before she reached them there was a sudden commotion at the door.

Conversations died as everyone turned to see what was happening. Alex recognized the voice of the new arrival, deep, resonant, unperturbed, even before she turned around and saw Will O'Keefe. He wore his faded cords and a carefully pressed cotton shirt, complete with tie, but *sans* jacket. On his feet were well-worn running shoes. He said, clearly and distinctly, "The ticket I bought said nothing about mandatory monkey suits."

A hushed, expectant silence fell, almost as though he were the entertainment for the evening. Alex felt both admiration for his guts and a strange protectiveness toward him. Before she realized what she was doing, she moved toward him.

Rodney followed, hissing in her ear, "Let the butler handle this."

Marvin, their surfer-butler, was attempting to shove Will back out into the hall. Will stood his ground and said levelly, "I suggest you keep your hands to yourself and go and fetch our hostess. I want to hear from her that my hundred-dollar ticket is no good."

Several photographers materialized, cameras snapping, lights flashing. Only the elderly photographer who represented the Sand Point *Bulletin* kept a respectful distance.

Alex reached Will's side just ahead of Amelia, and announced in ringing tones, "Really, Marvin, you can see that Mr. O'Keefe has a perfectly legitimate ticket and this *is* a fund-raising evening. I'm sure all the poor stray animals we're trying to help don't care how Mr. O'Keefe is dressed, do they, Amelia?"

Amelia's mouth opened but nothing came out. She gave Alex a withering stare. Her husband, Bart, with a politician's aplomb, gestured for the musicians, who were waiting on a dais at the end of the room, to begin playing. Then he scurried over to Amelia and drew her arm through his. "Come along, my dear, we must lead the dancing." Without moving his lips, he added under his breath to Will, "You're going to regret this, my friend." To the hovering newsmen, he said, "Just a little misunderstanding, boys, of course, every animal-lover is welcome here."

Rodney said coldly, "I really don't know why some people must push themselves where they're not wanted. Alex, let's dance, shall we?"

She had time to give Will an encouraging smile before Rodney dragged her toward the square of polished parquet that had been cleared for dancing. As she followed Rodney's carefully precise lead—he repeated the same steps in exactly the same way throughout the dance—Alex saw Will standing on the sidelines, munching on caviar and pâté. He raised a glass of champagne in her direction and winked.

Funny how just Will's presence filled her with courage, Alex thought. She smiled at him over Rodney's shoulder.

When the music ended Amelia stalked them through the thronging guests. "I'm quite disappointed in you, Alex. First you arrive looking like a . . . a . . . well, I don't care to say what you look like in that disgraceful outfit. Then you help that awful man spoil my whole evening. I wonder if you and he planned to humiliate me in front of all my friends."

"Mother . . ." Rodney began ingratiatingly.

She silenced him in short order. "You . . . you fool, why did you bring her here dressed like that? Go and dance with Miss Munro's niece."

Rodney dutifully loped off in search of Gigi Munro, who despite her giddy name was a mousy young woman clad in a dress more suitable for a dowager than an eighteen-year-old. Of all of the families in town, Alex knew that the Barringtons stood only in awe of the Munros, who were "old money" and whose family name could be traced back to Jamestown. Gigi, the spinster sisters' niece, had recently arrived from Vassar to spend her summer vacation with her aunts.

Amelia added, "I suggest you make as discreet an exit as possible, Alex. If you wish to change into something more suitable for the occasion, you may return. Otherwise . . ."

"Oh, I'm quite comfortable, Amelia," Alex responded

sweetly. "I think I'd like some more champagne before I go." She strode off on her four-and-a-half-inch heels, showing Amelia her bare back and waylaid the nearest waiter.

She had downed another glass when a voice at her side said, "Bravo, there's hope for you yet, Alex."

"I can't believe you'd spend a hundred dollars to come here," Alex snapped. "What did you hock? Your boat? And just what are you trying to prove?"

"Oh, I don't know . . . that all dogs like all men are born equal, perhaps? Or maybe I just don't like being told what I can or cannot do. I never did believe in submitting to dictators."

Will's dark eyes were filled with amusement. He gently removed the empty glass from her hand and slipped his arm around her waist. "Come on, let's dance. I watched with dread as you went around the floor with Rodney. I was sure that thing you're wearing was going to fall off you. How do you keep it on, anyway?"

Alex was beginning to feel the effects of the unaccustomed champagne. It was a relief to relax against Will and let him guide her. The combo was now playing a slow piece and with her high heels, Alex found her head rested very comfortably against Will's shoulder. They swayed together in sweetly sensuous harmony, not speaking, yet fully aware of the messages their bodies transmitted to one another.

When the music stopped one of the Misses Munro, her eyes twinkling merrily, tapped Alex on the shoulder. "My dear, I don't know if my sister thanked you properly for finding Frances for us the other day. We are so grateful."

"Oh, think nothing of it, Miss Munro."

"I love your jumpsuit," the old lady went on. "So

bright and colorful. One gets so tired of pastel satins and laces. I do wish Gigi had your flair. Such a little mouse." She peered up at Will near-sightedly.

"Oh, forgive me, Miss Munro, may I present Will O'Keefe."

Will cradled the wrinkled old hand in his as though it were a rare jewel. "We met briefly at the pet hospital, Miss Munro. You had Ambrose with you."

"Such a naughty boy. Alex, I don't suppose there's any way we can make him stop using those awful words, is there?"

"Not that I know of—" Alex began, when there was a drum-roll and Amelia Barrington took the microphone.

"Ladies and gentlemen, before we go to the buffet tables, I'd like to thank you all for coming tonight to support our cause. I don't have to remind anyone here of the tragedy of unwanted animals or the irresponsibility of those who allow their pets to breed indiscriminately. Let me instead state that we here this evening are looking forward to a world where every pet is wanted, where every puppy born is the result of careful breeding."

She paused, and there was a smattering of applause which ended when Will's voice asked, "Mrs. Barrington, there's a big difference between curing the problem of unwanted pets and eliminating from the earth all varieties of animal that don't measure up to your particular standards of elegance. I believe in the Third Reich Adolf Hitler had similar ideas to yours. It didn't work for people either."

A gasp rustled through the audience and several cameras popped in Will's direction. At his side, Alex thought, now he's done it. Her champagne-induced euphoria fled, leaving her all too aware of her own vulnerability, yet, surprisingly, proud of Will and proud that she was with him.

Will went on, "I'd like to add that I trust my own donation to tonight's shindig will be used for the proposed animal shelter, not to implement some piece of tomfool legislation. Now, having had my say, I'll bid you all good night." He gently slid Alex's arm from his. "Enjoy the party, Dr. Aimes. Thanks for the dance."

He had started to walk toward the door before Alex came to her senses. She could see Amelia staring at her, her expression saying clearly that if Alex left now she was finished in Sand Point.

Not that Will expected her to go, he'd made that clear. In fact, he expected her to stay. He certainly wouldn't want her to give up a prospering practice for the sake of making some idealistic statement that wasn't even necessary since surely Bart Barrington would never actually present such a ridiculous bill to the state legislature.

"Will!" Alex called, running after him. "Wait for me."

7

~oooooooooooooo~

Standing among the parked cars, Will grinned at Alex. "Well, now, having made our grand gesture, we seem to be left without a means of escape. You came in Rodney's car and I came on my bike."

Alex shrugged, "I'll ride on the handlebars. Just be careful going down the hill, okay?"

"Alex, I don't know what caused this transformation in you. I was intrigued by you before but now I think I'm overwhelmed by you. You've shown a side of yourself tonight I wouldn't have believed you'd possessed."

"Oh, it was there all the time. I just have to fight to keep it hidden."

He retrieved his bike from the bushes, positioned himself on the seat and Alex on the crossbar, enclosed by his arms.

The ride down the hill with the ocean breeze in their faces was exhilarating. Just like being carried off on the horse of a gallant knight, Alex decided, as she leaned back against Will's chest and her hair flew in every direction.

For the first time in years Alex felt young, unencumbered, recklessly daring. She was also beginning to feel a stirring of another more primitive emotion as she pressed herself back against Will and felt his warm breath against her hair. She looked down at his arms, muscles taut as he steered the bike, aware of the strength of his hands with their broad-tipped fingers, and imagined those hands caressing her as she lay within the circle of his arms.

Over the ocean the last scarlet streaks of the sunset faded into a night sky that promised a million stars. There was a gentle quality to the air that said summer was almost here and it was time to fulfill winter dreams.

Now why had that thought popped unbidden into her mind? Had she been dreaming of romance? Surely not Alex Aimes—she of the iron will and steely determination to be absolutely secure in her career before choosing, with the utmost care, an acquiescent husband and perfect father for her future children. He would, of course, have to defer to her career and lifestyle.

The thought that the man who had just nuzzled her hair aside to impulsively place a kiss on the nape of her neck could even be considered for the role, was utterly ridiculous. Will O'Keefe would never defer to any woman . . . or man, for that matter.

So why did she feel a long sigh escape from parted lips, and a certain tension in the region of her breasts as thin silk tightened against her nipples?

When at last Will pedaled up the steep incline toward her cottage and came to a stop at the gate, Alex was beyond reasoning or analyzing her churning emotions.

She felt his hands grip her waist as he set her gently down on the ground, and immediately turned to face him, placing her hands on his chest. She looked up at him through the deepening twilight, unsure what she was about to say until the words fell softly between them. "Would you . . . please kiss me?"

His lips were warm, pulsing with a life force that called insistently to some answering chord in her, and his tongue found a willing companion in hers. She wanted to surrender to all of the sensations that hovered within reach, feeling a delicious lethargy steal over her body as she seemed to float, weightless, supported only by his touch. But Red's insistent barking broke the spell.

Will chuckled as he released her. "Come on, I know exactly how to take care of your friend Red."

They went into the darkened house and as the setter rushed about them in excited circles Will commanded, "Come on, Red. Your lady friend is waiting for you down on the beach." He opened the back door and went outside, Red obediently at his heels.

Alex stood and watched as if in a trance, until moments later Will returned. He moved toward her, slipped his arms around her and, kissing her lightly, raised her a few inches from the floor. He walked slowly, carrying her, nibbling her lower lip. The floating sensation returned, stronger than ever.

Nudging open the bedroom door with his knee, he suddenly swung her up into his arms, impatient to place her on the bed. Silver light spilled into the room as an almost-full moon sailed into view of the open window.

She lay back and watched as he tore off his own clothes, then bent over her with a gentler touch to remove hers. Easing the fragile silk jumpsuit down over her body, hooking his fingers carefully into her lacy panties, his breathing grew steadily more labored.

"You're so beautiful, Alex . . . I'm out of my mind wanting you, yet suddenly I feel as clumsy as a boy. I've never made love to a woman I cared so much about before."

"I know," she whispered. "Will, I want you to make love to me. I feel as if I've wanted it for a very long time."

She raised her arms in order to clasp her hands about his neck, feeling the strength of his body and the powerful surging of his desire as he swung himself over her, supported by his hands.

At first he was almost too gentle, too tentative, as though he felt she were too delicate a receptacle for the intensity of his need. One hand went under her, cupping her buttocks to raise her body to meet his. She felt herself mold to fit perfectly against masculine planes and hollows, her breasts crushed against a soft mat of pectoral hair, her thighs forming a yielding cushion for him.

She writhed uncontrollably as his hands explored her now, followed quickly by his lips, raining soft kisses on inflamed flesh, circling the erect peaks of her nipples.

Seizing his head in her hands, she gasped her pleasure and cried out her need for even deeper caresses. "Darling . . . Will . . . please, I want to feel you inside me."

Now his passion was at full floodtide and could no longer be contained. He parted her thighs and she guided him as their bodies seemed to dissolve into rushing waves and exploding lights.

There had never been such joy, so wild, so utterly

harmonious. There was giving and taking, anticipating and needing, being one yet feeling separate pleasures, her own and his.

Then they were rushing toward some unseen pinnacle of sensation and nothing could prevent their reaching an ecstasy that was both a distant fusion of two comets and a sweet earthy union of two mortal beings.

When at last they lay spent in each other's arms and the moonlight etched his rugged features into sharp relief, Alex saw to her surprise that his face, stripped of all but a wonder that she herself felt acutely, was much more handsome than she'd realized.

Sighing softly, she ran her hands over his chest, loving the strength and power she felt in his body, feeling utterly protected by it. "Oh, Will . . ." she said, and nestling closer, drifted off to sleep.

Will watched her sleeping, her cheek pale against his tanned shoulder, her hair a silken curtain that smelled as sweet as newly opened blossoms. Already he wanted her again, and he had to ease his lower body away from the curve of her thigh so that he wouldn't awaken her. Her softly rounded breasts rose and fell against his chest, tempting and tantalizing, yet he resisted the urge to touch them, to trace their perfection with his fingertip.

Still overwhelmed by the intensity of his emotions, he asked himself wryly why he had never before experienced such an afterglow. There had been women he might have loved, and women he had made love to, but somehow they were in two different worlds. Now that he had met Alex he was both eager and yet hesitant, unsure if feelings this all-engrossing could possibly last. Surely such a flame would consume itself with its own heat?

What does she see in me, he asked himself as he stroked a strand of hair back from her eyes. Am I merely an interesting unkempt stranger passing through her ordered world? A diversion, good for an interlude, to be filed away later in memory? All she knows of me is that I'm totally unsuitable to settle in a place like Sand Point, living the life she's chosen. And what about my own needs in a woman? Doctor Aimes, respected veterinarian who hobnobs with the super-rich, is probably slightly to the right of Genghis Khan when it comes to politics. Could I really expect such a woman to follow my lifestyle?

No, we both were carried away by rampaging hormones, that's all. After tonight I'd better beat a hasty retreat. Discretion being the better part of valor. Keep telling yourself, Will my lad, that it's all purely physical.

Alex stirred against him, bringing her sweet curves into closer contact with his sensitive flesh. Without conscious effort, his hand began to drift down her back, around her small waist, upward to cup her breast, surprisingly full for one so slender. He pressed his lips to her forehead, moved to kiss her eyelids. Her lashes fluttered against his mouth like awakening birds and he took her lips, drawing them to his and tasting her sweetness.

Her scent filled his nostrils and he trembled as he gathered her closer into his arms. In her completely relaxed state she seemed so vulnerable, so infinitely pliable and yielding, that it was difficult for him to realize that the woman in his arms was the same self-possessed, bright, businesslike veterinarian who had been so outraged that her Irish setter had coupled with his retriever. Yet wasn't that what made Alex so exciting? Her self-confidence, her maturity, her independence, and under it all, a warm and loving woman in every sense of the word?

"Will . . ." she murmured, her voice drugged with sleep.

"Yes," he answered softly, "I'm still here. Still wanting you. Sorry I didn't mean to wake you."

For an answer her hand trailed down his chest, exploring his body with a soft, wondering touch. When she spoke, he felt perhaps the statement came from that half-awake state of awareness where feeling is more important than reasoning. She said, "How wonderful to wake up to the promise of passion."

As he bent to take her nipple into his mouth he thought it wise to not read more into her words than her fully-awake self would want him to do. Nor should he make any declaration to her that would be regretted by both of them in the cold light of reality.

8

Alex awoke feeling wonderfully light and airy, as though she could fly out of the open window and soar over the Pacific into the cloudless sky. It was several minutes before she became aware of two important facts.

First, that Will was no longer beside her in bed, although she remembered how it had been to fall asleep after the second time they made love, paradoxically, both thrilling and soothing. And secondly the heavenly aroma of crisping bacon drifted into the room, bringing her fully awake and ravenous.

She showered and slipped into shorts and tee shirt, then, barefoot and with wet hair, went into the kitchen where Will stood at the stove. He gave her his slow and easy smile, dropped the spatula and opened his arms in invitation. "Thought the smell of bacon would get you. Come here and give me a hug."

His kiss was gentle, his arms felt as though they

belonged around her. How easy it would be to get used to this, Alex thought. She murmured, "I'm starving, how about you?"

Will turned her around to face the table. Freshly-squeezed orange juice and a pot of coffee were waiting. He'd set the table with her best linen cloth and china and picked one of her early roses for the centerpiece.

"Very nice," Alex said, then sipped from a glass of juice. "You're a handy man to have around. But I was really hoping for breakfast on a white wicker tray in bed."

"I didn't dare," Will answered, bringing a platter of bacon and glistening slices of broiled tomato to the table. "If I'd come back into the bedroom the day would have been shot and I've got to get into town to the post office and mail an article today if I'm to meet my deadline. That is, after I finish typing it."

"This is an interesting combination," Alex remarked, looking at the bacon and tomato.

"A habit I picked up in England. Now there's a nation that really knows how to put a breakfast together. You didn't have any mushrooms, bangers or kidneys though."

"How little I know about you. You've traveled quite extensively, I suppose?"

"Seen most of the world." His smile faded, replaced by a thoughtful expression.

"And?" Alex prompted.

"Oh, nothing. I was just thinking that you've probably seen very little of the world outside of medical school and Sand Point. Just one more difference between us. Who-ever commented that opposites attract must have had you and I in mind."

Alex's fork suddenly clattered to her plate. "Oh, no!"

"Well, it isn't a monumental problem—" Will began.

"I just remembered we walked out on Amelia Barrington last night."

"Calm down, kid. It was time. Now you'll find out that you can make it without being sponsored by the Barringtons."

"I hope you're right. You know, it's just occurred to me—it's Sunday today. The post office won't be open."

"Not in Sand Point, but I can drive over to the main post office, weigh the package and get stamps from the machine. It'll give me a day's start on mail going out from here."

Alex regarded him silently for a moment. Was there a wary look in his eyes that hadn't been there before? "I wasn't trying to keep you here," she said defensively. "As a matter of fact I have to go to the hospital and take care of the animals anyway. Weekends just mean no appointments with human owners for me."

"Look, I'll be as fast as I can and try to be back this afternoon so we can have a couple of hours on the beach together."

She stood up. "Don't do me any favors."

"Now what brought on this sudden change of mood? What do you mean?"

"Nothing. I didn't expect you to hang around here all day waiting on me. There was no need to think up excuses to leave." She began to gather up the dishes and carry them to the sink.

Will came behind her, slipped his arms around her and kissed the nape of her neck. "It wasn't an excuse. I do have a deadline. I'd much prefer to spend the day with you, but Meggie and I like to eat occasionally, and I make my living from my writing."

"The dogs!" Alex exclaimed. "I haven't given them fresh water."

He turned her around to face him. "I did. They're fine."

"They were on the beach all night too," Alex said. "What was I thinking of?"

"The cove is so sheltered, what harm would come to them?"

"For one thing, dogs aren't supposed to run loose on the beaches in Sand Point. This beach is tiny and inaccessible but knowing how vindictive Amelia Barrington can be, I think it would be a good idea not to break *any* laws when it comes to the dogs."

"You're probably right. I'll bring Red up and then take Meggie back to the boat with me. And Alex, quit frowning. We had a wonderful night together last night, let's not spoil it by making unrealistic demands on each other, okay? We're still the same two people we were yesterday afternoon."

She pulled free of his arms. "My sentiments exactly. You'd better go and write your article."

"I'll bring some steaks back for dinner, okay?"

"No, you can't afford to," she began, thinking of the hundred-dollar ticket he'd bought for the Barringtons' ball.

Thunderclouds raced across Will's eyes. "Don't tell me what I can and cannot afford."

"I just meant—"

"I'll see you later, Alex. I forgot to mention—when I cook, you do the dishes."

The house seemed lonely after Will left. Red Baron moped too, regarding Alex with accusing brown eyes, until she said, "Oh, all right. You can come into town with me. But no agitating the other dogs, okay? I don't want any jailbreaks on my hands nor any riots. They're in the cages for very good reasons."

Red wagged his tail and gave a doggy smile.

They were on their way out to the car when a rusting Chevy came laboring up the hill, gears grinding and a trail of oil in its wake.

Alex put Red into her car and closed the door. The Chevy looked vaguely familiar. As it drew closer she recognized the driver. Cosmo. The ancient merchant mariner who had tried to set up a fish taco stand in Sand Point.

He beamed at her out of the open driver's window as the car wheezed to a halt. "Never thought we'd make it up that hill. Howdy, Doc."

"Hi, Cosmo. What are you doing in these parts?"

"Looking for you, little lady. I just wanted to be sure you got Frances back to Miz Munro, okay. I felt bad after I left you, in case that mutt gave you a hard time. Shoulda stayed and took care of her myself, but there was so many officials insisting I get outa town."

Alex smiled. "Frances is safely home. How very nice of you to care. I was just going to check on the animals in the hospital, but I've got time to make you a cup of coffee first. Come on in."

"Oh, no thanks, Doc. I've got to be on my way. My friend is expecting me back."

"You have a place to stay, then? I'm so glad. Be sure and let me know if you ever start selling those wonderful fish tacos again."

"Uh huh. Maybe sometime we could get together and have a picnic? Maybe I'd even get my friend to join us."

"Why, thank you, Cosmo. That would be very nice."

"Uh . . . er . . . you found Miz Munro well, then? Not too worried about the dog?"

"She was fine. I didn't see her sister, but I'm sure they're both very grateful to you."

Something clicked in the back of Alex's mind, a half-formed idea she didn't have time to express as Cosmo waved goodbye and roared off down the hill.

On her way into town she remembered the way the uncontrollable Frances had groveled at Cosmo's feet and obeyed his commands. She also recalled that Cosmo had first been seen around Sand Point—although not selling tacos—around about the time the Misses Munro acquired both Frances and the parrot, Ambrose. Cosmo had been a sailor. Wasn't a parrot the traditional pet of the sailor? Wasn't the parrot's salty language an indication of a past life among men, rather than women?

Intrigued by the possibilities conjured up by her speculation, Alex wasn't aware of the highway patrol car behind her until the blinking red light in her rearview mirror caught her attention.

She pulled over and waited for the officer to appear at her window, sure he was only about to point out a missing taillight or some other minor infraction. Instead, she listened incredulously as he pointed out that she had been speeding.

"I couldn't have been doing more than thirty," she protested.

"In a twenty-five-mile zone," he responded, and proceeded to write the ticket.

Surely, she thought, the Barringtons haven't had time to put out the word already?

The day was fast losing its gloss.

There was worse to come. When she arrived at the pet hospital Juan was just finishing cleaning the dog runs. He avoided her eyes as he mumbled, "I'm sorry, *señorita*. I can't work for you no more after today."

The knot of tension between her brow tightened another notch. "But why? Can we talk about it. Is it the hours, or the pay—"

"No, *señorita*. I got a better job. My family needs the money."

"Of course, I understand. Where will you be working?"

He raked the dirt furiously. "At some stables, looking after the horses."

"The Barringtons' stables?" Alex asked. "Looking after polo ponies?"

There was no need for him to reply, his shamefaced expression told it all. She went back to the cages where the sick animals were kept in isolation, wondering if it would do her any good to call the high school to see if any other student wanted a job.

Juan followed, shuffling his feet and staring at the floor. Alex said, "I'll get your paycheck ready as soon as I've checked the surgery patients."

"No hurry. I forgot to tell you, Miss Munro called. She wants to talk to you."

Why was it that doctors and vets weren't supposed to take Sundays off, she wondered, but made the call to the Munro mansion as soon as she'd finished her rounds.

Alex was so dispirited by now that she half expected to hear that her services in connection with Frances and Ambrose would no longer be required.

Instead one of the Misses Munro said, "We're so sorry to trouble you on a Sunday, Alex, but as you know, our

81

niece is spending a couple of weeks with us and we wondered if it would be possible to board Ambrose with you while she's here. We feel so embarrassed by the things he says. Certainly the words and expressions he uses shouldn't be heard by an impressionable young girl."

Smothering a smile at the notion that any of today's young girls could be so sheltered, Alex replied, "Of course, I'd be glad to take care of him. Would you like to bring him in today?"

"Yes, that would be fine. We'll bring him in after church."

"After church" proved to be in the middle of the afternoon. Alex wondered if Will had returned from the post office and was waiting for her on the beach. It would seem that she was deliberately staying away to punish him for walking out on her this morning. Why did circumstances always seem to conspire to give the wrong impression?

The Munros' well-polished sedan arrived just before three o'clock. The sisters, in identical dusty pink suits with black straw hats, alighted from the back seat of the car while their chauffeur lifted Ambrose's wrought-iron cage from the front seat.

"Get Frances!" Ambrose screamed. "Where's that sucker?"

"Just put him on the counter," Alex told the chauffeur.

"Such a naughty boy," one Miss Munro said.

"He is so attached to Frances," the other one said. "Would it be all right if we brought Frances in to visit Ambrose while he's here?"

"Yes, of course." Alex held open the door to the waiting room so that the group could go inside. "There's a form to sign and I'd like to discuss Ambrose's diet with you before you leave."

Outside on the street a bike came whizzing up, stopping just short of the Munro car. Will O'Keefe jumped to the curb and burst into the waiting room. He was breathing heavily and there was something almost akin to fear in his eyes.

Alex looked up in surprise.

"Trouble," Will said. He glanced at the maiden ladies, bowed slightly and said, "Good afternoon, would you excuse us for a moment?"

Alex opened the door to the examining room and motioned for Will to follow her inside.

"Oh, God, Alex, I was a fool!"

"What are you trying to tell me?"

"I finished the article this morning, got back from the main post office by noon. I waited, but you didn't show. I'd bought steaks, but I thought it would be nice to get a good bottle of wine to go with them."

Alex felt an icy finger of fear, knowing what was coming.

Will went on. "I left Meggie on the beach while I rode the bike to town. When I got back she was gone."

9

—◦◦◦◦◦◦◦◦◦◦—

Somehow Alex got the Misses Munro out of the waiting room, locked the door and pulled the shade. "Did you search for Meggie?"

"Everywhere, all over the beach, into the next cove along the bluff, the highway. Your yard. She's gone and I know she wouldn't just wander off without me, she never has. Somebody took her."

"Will," Alex said gently, "it's pretty unlikely. The cottage and the beach are way off the beaten track and nobody knew Meggie was loose on the beach there."

"Only the Barringtons," Will said grimly.

Alex had told Amelia, of course, about Red Baron's encounter with the Golden Retriever. Alex instantly felt guilty. "If they sent the dog catcher out, then she's been taken to the pound. There isn't one in Sand Point, the nearest is over in Emerald Quay. It won't be open to the public until tomorrow morning."

Will paced a small circle around the waiting room. "Damn, I shouldn't have left her loose like that. But I was only gone fifteen minutes."

"Put your bike in the shed out back and we'll drive back to the cottage and search some more. There are some caves on the far side of the cove that are hard to see from the beach because they're hidden by the offshore rocks."

They spent the rest of the afternoon and early evening combing beaches, bluffs and caves for Meggie. Red Baron accompanied them and Alex was sure from his anxious prancing that he knew what was wrong.

The caves on the far side of the cove were accessible by land only at low tide when a narrow strip of beach appeared, and since there was a high tide that afternoon, they went in Will's dinghy. As he carefully negotiated the jagged entrance to the caves, Alex caught his arm. "Look, over there."

A rubber dinghy was tied to one of the rocks, floating up with the rising tide to a high and dry ledge where they could see camping equipment. A rolled sleeping bag, several cardboard boxes, a camp stove.

"Wonder how long there's been a tenant here?" Will asked, his voice echoing hollowly about the cave.

"Not long. Red and I were over here a week or two ago at low tide. I hope he's aware that if there's a hurricane off the Baja this cave fills almost to the roof in the high surf. We can get fifteen-foot breakers on the south facing beaches."

"Let's get out of here. Meggie isn't here. I'll come back later and see if I can find the camper; maybe he saw her."

When dusk fell and there was still no sign of the missing retriever, Will reluctantly suggested they give up.

Returning to the cottage, Alex reflected silently that tonight's homecoming was vastly different from the previous evening, when the sexual tension between them had eclipsed everything else. Although Will tried valiantly to make small talk and proudly showed her the wine he'd bought, and the steaks that had ingeniously been kept cool inside a clay plant pot he'd immersed in water, she was well aware of his anxiety about his pet.

Together they prepared dinner, Will barbecuing the steaks while she tossed a salad. After they'd eaten and cleared the dishes, Will decided to go back to the cave to see if the camper had returned.

Half an hour later he came back and told her the dinghy and other items were still there, but there was no sign of the camper.

They went outside and sat out on the deck, ostensibly to sip wine and enjoy the balmy air, but really to watch the beach below in case Meggie returned.

Alex reached out and placed her hand over Will's, giving it a reassuring squeeze. "She's in the pound at Emerald Quay. Don't worry. We'll get her out as soon as they open in the morning."

He turned to look at her. "You're a helluva nice person, Alex Aimes."

"I love my dog too, I know what you must be going through."

"I wasn't referring just to your support today." He stared into the vast darkness of the sea, which churned restlessly against the shore.

After a moment he added, "I really didn't intend to stay here, you know. Not after my article on affordable housing was completed. I'd researched it in several California communities. Sand Point was just one I selected. Oh, I knew it was Barrington turf, of course, and I suppose that influenced my choice. Old Bart is a crooked politician who has his eye on the governor's mansion. I'd hate to see him make it, but I really just came here to do the article."

Alex sighed. "Instead you met me and Red Baron. You must really be cursing the whims of fate. First we get Meggie pregnant, then . . ."

Will gave a ghost of a smile. "Oh, I'm not afraid you'll get me pregnant."

Alex laughed, feeling some of the tension disappear. Impulsively she said, "Stay here with me tonight, Will. No strings, no ulterior motives. Just cuddle up in bed with me and let me hold you. I don't think you should go back to your boat alone."

"Thought you'd never ask," he answered, grinning. "How about a moonlight dip in the ocean first? I feel the need to do something physical to take my mind off Meggie."

Although she found a darkened sea more than a little terrifying, as thoughts of sharks in feeding frenzies hovered, Alex nodded and went into the bedroom to slip into an ancient one-piece swimsuit.

When she reappeared on the deck Will gave her an amused smile. "You really think you need that suit? There's just us. I don't have trunks with me."

"Old habits die hard," Alex said lightly. She could have added that skinny-dipping seemed provocative, in view of her earlier statement. Her feelings toward Will were still so ambivalent it was difficult to make sense of them.

"That suit looks like something your high school gym teacher insisted on."

"I didn't know you were an expert on beach bunnies. But then, there's so much I don't know about you, isn't there?" A defensive note had crept back into her tone and she was annoyed with him for causing her to feel that way.

"What do you want to know about me?"

"Where did you go to school?"

He surveyed her silently for a moment, his face illuminated only by the yellow glow of a lantern over the back door of the cottage. "That's very important to you, isn't it? The right school, a proper education. Tell me, where do you draw the line? Masters' degrees? Doctorates? Don't be an education snob, Alex. You'll eliminate a lot of interesting people from your life if you are. It's just as bad as being the kind of *nouveau riche* snobs the Barringtons are."

"Dammit, don't criticize me," Alex said angrily. "I asked a simple question and I get a lecture instead of an answer."

"The simple question had undertones I didn't care for. I'm sorry if I lectured though. Come on, we both need to cool off."

He tried to take her hand to lead her down the steep steps cut into the cliff, but she evaded him and, knowing the way better than he, ran ahead of him.

When they reached the beach he stripped off his clothes and left them on a rock. Alex, still smarting, raced toward the crashing surf. He caught up with her as she reached the shallows.

Diving under the first wave, she felt the frightening thrill of stingingly cold water driven by powerful swells that crashed against the shore in exploding sprays of phosphorescence. She surfaced on the far side of the breaker to see Will's head a few feet away.

"Catch the next one," he shouted over the roar of the surf.

There was no time to explain that she had never learned the tricky art of body-surfing. In a life dedicated to study and work, her playtime hours had been too few. Besides, she was still too angry to admit there was something she couldn't do. As the incoming wave towered over her, Will yelled, "Now!"

Closing her eyes, she put down her head and dove with the wave. She felt herself picked up, caught in the rushing force of the sea, then she was sliding down the front of the wave, not swimming, not floating, practically flying.

The ride to shore, at the speed of a freight train, was wildly exhilarating. Alex found herself in the shallows, rolling in the sand churned up by the breaking wave, laughing and choking and spitting saltwater, her anger dissipated in the sparkling foam.

Strong arms went under her and she was hauled to her feet and held in a bear hug. Will said, "I always promised myself if I ever found a woman who could bodysurf—"

"Don't be too reckless with the promises. I forgot to tell you, I don't know how. Oh, I've watched other people do it but that was the first wave I ever rode."

Will threw back his head and laughed the full-bodied laugh she loved. "Good for you! At night, yet! Want to try it again?"

"Of course, come on."

The first ride must have been a lucky fluke, she decided, when her next attempt wiped her out. She tumbled to shore, head over heels, and came up gasping for breath. Will scraped her up off the bottom and carried her to dry sand. He laid her down gently, stretched out beside her and pulled her into his arms.

"You got a little over-confident. Timing is everything when you're surfing. You went too late on that one."

She began to shiver as the night air found wet skin. "Maybe I'll try again in the sunlight."

"Good idea. Come on, let's get you into a hot shower."

Aware all at once of the proximity of his powerful body, naked and glistening in the moonlight, Alex felt a spark ignite inside her. And yes, there was plenty of room for two in the cottage shower.

Will stood up and offered his hand to help her to her feet.

As she rose she felt something slide between her toes. Bending to remove it, she knew what it was the moment she touched the damp leather. Wordlessly she held up the dog collar, with its rabies tag and oval brass plate bearing the name *Meggie*.

They went through the pathetic line of dog cages at the Emerald Quay Animal Shelter for a third time. The lost and abandoned dogs either barked furiously, or wagged tails hopefully. A few slept, either indifferent or too dispirited to care. Meggie was not one of them.

One of the attendants said encouragingly, "It's early yet. Perhaps the animal control officer hasn't brought your dog in yet."

Walking back out to the car park, Alex said, "There are other animal shelters. This is the closest to Sand Point, but that doesn't mean—"

"Meggie didn't drown," Will said, staring straight ahead. "She's a good swimmer and she's swum from boat to shore and back many times."

"No, of course she didn't drown. Probably her collar came off in the struggle as she resisted arrest."

Will was too desolate to smile at her attempt at humor. As they reached her car he said savagely, "I'd like to borrow your car and drive out to the Barringtons. By God, I'll make them tell me where she is."

Alex looked at the set of his jaw, the way his knuckles showed white as he grasped the door handle, and the set of his powerful shoulders. In his present state of anger and anxiety he was probably capable of tearing all three Barringtons limb from limb, she decided. "No Will. Let's go back to my office and we'll call every pound in the county until we find her."

"And you think she's the only Golden Retriever that's been picked up? They took her collar and ID off, remember? If she was taken in yesterday that means she's already in day two of her death sentence. After three days if they aren't picked up by their owners or adopted, they're put down. With at least an hour's drive from one town to another, time for checking every dog they've got and having to do it all before four in the afternoon, we could run out of time. I can't take the chance."

"Will, I can't let you have my car in your present state of mind. I'm sorry. I'm going to go back to Sand Point and start making calls."

"Fine. I'll ride back with you and get my bike."

There was little conversation on the way back. Alex glanced at her watch and saw that she'd be late for her first appointment of the day. Somehow she'd have to make calls to the various animal shelters between patients today. She wondered if by tonight she might also be trying to bail Meggie's owner out of the town jail.

She saw when they arrived that her fears about being late to open the pet hospital were unfounded. There were no patients waiting to get in. She opened the waiting room and went straight to the phone. Will went around back to collect his bike and she saw him pedal away as the first animal shelter responded to her call. They had two Golden Retrievers, a puppy and an elderly male. She hung up and dialed again.

"Avast, you lubber," a muffled voice squawked. "Off with the clothes." Alex reached over and pulled the cover from Ambrose's cage. He gave her an indignant stare and ruffled his gaudy feathers.

Some of the lines were busy and she had to dial several times. Halfway through the morning she realized that not a single appointment had been kept that morning. Nor had anyone called to cancel, but of course, she'd kept the line tied up. Will had not returned.

Ambrose kept up a steady stream of obscenities, interspersed with some comical phrases. Someone had taken a great deal of time to teach the parrot such a large, if tainted, vocabulary. There was a strong seafaring flavor, sometimes archaic, to the bird's conversation.

The mail carrier arrived just before noon, bringing a certified letter for her. She signed for it and tore it open. It was a formal thirty-day notice to vacate property. The Barringtons wanted her out of the beach cottage as it was "needed for a family member."

At least they couldn't ask her to get out of the pet hospital; she had eight months to go on her year's lease.

But the cottage had been rented on a monthly basis. It was probably all academic anyway, since if she had no patients she wouldn't be able to pay the rent on the hospital.

There was only one animal shelter left that she hadn't reached. She picked up the phone, then saw the battered Chevy slide to a stop in front of the building. Cosmo was at the wheel and, seated beside him was a familiar dog.

Alex rushed outside. Cosmo was halfway out of the car. "Couldn't get you on the phone. Your line was busy."

"Meggie!" Alex exclaimed, flinging her arms around the retriever, who thumped her tail and nuzzled Alex's neck. "Oh, you bad girl, where have you been?"

Cosmo came around the car and lifted Meggie out. He carried her into the waiting room and Alex followed.

"She's okay, Doc. I took good care of her. See I saw the dog catcher come down into the cove and try to grab her, only she slipped out of her collar and started to swim for the sloop. I lost sight of her and figured she'd made it all right. Only there was a strong riptide and I reckon she got caught in it and swept up the coast. I was out fishing this morning in my dinghy and I saw her on one of the offshore rocks. Fair wore out, she was."

"Your dinghy. So it was you camping in the caves across the cove? You old rascal, I thought you told me you were staying with a friend."

Grinning sheepishly, he said, "Been on my own too long, I reckon. Needed some alone time. Oh, I got a friend all right, and I'm welcome to stay with him. Just wanted a couple of days fishing by myself, that's all."

He had placed Meggie on a table and Alex examined

the retriever carefully. She'd scraped her pads badly, no doubt scrambling onto the rocks, but otherwise seemed unhurt.

As the first wave of relief subsided, Alex felt another stab of apprehension. "Oh, no! I'd forgotten. Will, her owner, he's gone to confront the Barringtons!"

10

Will was held at bay by the electronic gates of the Barrington estate. He was pacing angrily up and down as Alex's car arrived. Turning, he saw Meggie on the front seat beside her and relief and joy flooded over his face. Alex saw him mouth the words, "Thank God," as he came toward them.

There were several minutes of hugs and licks and explanations before Alex asked, "I take it you never got inside the gates?"

"No. But I threatened plenty before they stopped answering the intercom. A cop showed up, but he couldn't arrest me for trespassing because I wasn't on their property. He warned me about disturbing the peace and left. I tried to get up over the wall, but they've got broken glass embedded in the top. I figured sooner or later somebody would have to go through those gates, so I just planned to wait."

"Get in," Alex said. "You've done enough damage here and I've got to get back to town just in case a patient shows up. Cosmo is minding the store for me."

On the way back down the long winding road that led to the Barrington estate Alex told him about her eviction notice. He listened quietly as she mulled over possibilities. "I could perhaps clear out the storage room at the pet hospital and move in there though I'm sure there's probably some zoning restriction that forbids it. I can't afford to buy a house. Property in Sand Point is way out of my reach. There are some expensive apartment buildings, but they're owned by the Barringtons. I guess there's nothing much I can do but to move up the coast and commute every day."

"You're determined to keep your practice in Sand Point then?"

"I'm not going to let the Barringtons drive me out, that's for sure."

"Atta girl. You've overlooked one other place to hang your hat."

"Where? Cosmo's cave? It's already occupied."

"My boat."

She glanced sideways at him, trying to assess the offer. He went on, "We'd be pretty cramped, but if we stored most of your stuff at the hospital—"

"Will, wait a minute. Are you telling me you plan to stay here indefinitely?"

He didn't reply for a moment, as if considering the possibility. Alex held her breath, surprised at how much she wanted him to say yes, he was going to stay.

At last he answered, "No, I don't believe Sand Point is where I want to spend the rest of my life. But I'll probably be here at least for the summer, it's as good a place to work as any and I've a fairly long piece to finish up before fall. By then perhaps you'll have realized that you made a bad choice here."

"You just don't understand, do you?" Alex said heatedly. "I had to *buy* my professional practice here. I can't just pick up and move on like you with your have-typewriter-will-travel type of job."

"As long as you stay in this town, you're locked in to toeing a social line, Alex, and you know it. Do you want to toady to these upper-crust snobs forever? Sure, go ahead and fight the Barringtons now—never leave town with your tail between your legs—but for God's sake give some thought to a future somewhere else."

A future with you? She wanted to ask, but bit her tongue. That was no future for a veterinarian at all. She couldn't travel around as he did, and there was no way she was ever going to give up her profession. "The only future I'm concerned with right now is the end of the month and how I'll pay the bills if I don't have any patients."

They were still driving through Barrington land as the family owned several hundred acres surrounding their walled estate. The road curved around the edge of the hill, temporarily blocking the ocean view. The road straightened out again and Alex jammed on the brakes as a pack of hounds swarmed in front of her, followed by galloping horses.

"What the hell—" Will began, staring at the red-coated riders, one of whom yelled "Tally ho!" as she went by, her mount leaping across the ditch into the adjacent meadow. Somewhere to the rear of the group a hunting horn sounded, and the baying of the dogs drowned even the sound of thudding hooves.

"Riding pinks, hounds, am I dreaming, or are they fox-hunting?" Will said.

Before she could reply, a magnificent palomino appeared, with Rodney Barrington in the saddle. He recognized Alex's car in the split second before he urged the horse to jump the ditch and, jerking the reins abruptly as he turned to stare at Alex and Will, threw the palomino off balance. The horse crashed to the ground, hind legs in the ditch, and Rodney sailed over her head to sprawl in the long grass of the meadow.

The horse whinnied in pain, trying to pull himself up on his forelegs, but rolled back on the ground. Rodney was picking himself up and dusting himself off. Alex was out of the car, running, her medical bag in her hand, and she knew the horse's leg was broken before she reached the floundering animal.

"What can I do?" Will's voice was calm. He was at her side the instant she reached the injured horse.

"Hold his head, talk to him. Try to keep him still until I can give him a sedative. Then I'll set the leg." Will moved to follow her instructions and as she opened her bag and reached for a hypodermic needle Alex marveled at both his presence of mind and sheer strength as he held and calmed the horse.

The rest of the hunt had moved on, unaware of the small drama being played out on the road. Rodney came storming over to them. "Dammit, look what you did! Spooked my horse and now he's ruined. Broken leg. He'll have to be shot. I'm going to sue the hell out of you for this, O'Keefe."

Alex had administered the sedative and was now gently manipulating the broken bone. She looked up at Rodney's face, which was redder than his hunting jacket.

"It's a clean break, Rodney. There's no need to talk about destroying him. Even if you don't want to ride him again, although there's no reason you shouldn't, except for polo games, you can use him for stud purposes."

"You might as well leave him alone. I'm going home to get my gun and that animal is dead meat. When the courts get through awarding me damages, O'Keefe, you're going to be in hock forever."

"You've been seeing too many movies, Barrington," Will said quietly. "Only a fool would kill a valuable animal like this. Why don't you just shut up and let the doctor take care of him?"

Alex said, "We didn't spook the horse. I stopped the car long before you arrived. But take us to court, by all means. It's time somebody put a stop to your hunts. You've been hunting coyotes, haven't you? Letting the hounds tear the poor creature to pieces."

Rodney took a step backwards, some of his bluster dissipating. "We don't. We just ride with the hounds; we don't hunt coyotes."

Will said, "I've seen fox-hunting in England. Your hounds were in full cry. They weren't chasing thin air."

Rodney licked his lip nervously. "Alex—" he began.

"Take my car and go back to the house," Alex said curtly. "Get a horse trailer down here and be damn quick about it."

Rodney didn't need telling twice. The car made a fast U-turn and roared back up the road. Will gave Alex an appreciative smile. "Have I told you lately how much I admire you, Doc?"

"You're a pretty handy man to have around in an emergency yourself," Alex commented, aware with a sudden sense of longing that never before had there been someone at her side that she could count on, absolutely, unconditionally.

Alex lifted the bag of groceries out of the car and made her way toward the cottage. Meggie and Red, who had been sleeping together on the driveway, aroused themselves and came to greet her.

Meggie's pregnancy was now showing and Red was touchingly solicitous, always allowing Meggie to eat from his dish if she wished, to choose where to nap, even slowing his wild gallop along the beach to accommodate Meggie's now slower pace.

As she fondled first one dog and then the other with her free hand, Alex heard the staccato tapping of Will's typewriter coming from the open window of the cottage. He had moved in with her the day Rodney's horse had broken his leg. Alex had remarked, "Since I've only got the cottage for another month, if you'd like to work here . . . You might find it easier than bobbing around on the ocean."

They had an unspoken agreement that the arrangement was only temporary, Alex knew. She worried at how easily they had slipped into a life together, at how sweet it was. To make love before falling asleep, to swim together in the early morning, to have someone to talk to, to share with, someone waiting who was interested in everything that had happened while she'd been away from him.

It was too easy to get used to; unthinkable to live without, now that she'd had a sample of how it could be, living with a man. The right man. But of course, he wasn't right for her and never could be. This was temporary. She had to keep reminding herself.

The clicking typewriter keys stopped and Will opened the front door before she reached it, took her grocery bag from her and kissed her mouth with lingering precision. "I missed you, Alex. It's been a long day." He wore only a pair of faded swim trunks and Alex briefly caressed the taut, tanned flesh of his back before pulling away.

She fished in the bag and pulled out a glossy magazine. "Your article about affordable housing," she announced. "Look, you've got a cover blurb, and they used your photo of Sand Point. Now the fat's really going to be in the fire. Wait 'til the Barringtons read this. You've made them sound like feudal lords."

"Too bad I didn't know about their hunts when I wrote this," Will said, putting the groceries down on the table and taking the magazine from her. He flipped through it until he came to his article.

"We've no proof they hunt coyotes. And I don't know how anyone would get proof since they do it on their own land."

Will tossed the magazine down. "They cut my piece practically in half," he said disgustedly. He put his arms around her, then kissed her again. "How'd it go today?"

"Miss Munro came in and collected Ambrose. Her niece went back east. I'm going to miss that foul-mouthed bird. Oh yes, she brought Frances in for yet another check-up. I think the dear old soul feels I need the business, but actually I had several appointments today. Including Consuela's mother, who brought in Ramon. He'd been in another fight."

"What did she pay you with this time?"

"Homemade tortillas, they're in the grocery bag."

During the past couple of weeks it had quickly become

clear that the town was divided into two camps. The residents of the *barrio*, although they could ill-afford veterinary care for their pets, had made it a point to bring in their animals, paying a little cash, offering fresh vegetables and fruits when they had no money. It was a touching gesture that Alex knew probably wouldn't last after the first sense of outrage at the Barringtons passed.

More significantly, the Misses Munro and their friends had rallied behind Alex. And although the old guard of the town were fewer in number than the Barrington clique, and possessed a much smaller number of domestic pets, their business was enough to keep the pet hospital going.

"Cosmo is back in the cave," Will remarked as he began to unload the groceries. "I saw him today."

"I wonder where his friend lives," Alex mused. "Can't be too far away, that old Chevy of Cosmo's is only good for a short downhill run."

"A shack in one of the canyons, maybe?" Will suggested. "Plenty of places to hide away in the hills. Drill a well for water and get by with propane gas. I've done it myself."

"Have you now? I'm surprised you were able to stay in one place long enough to work for that newspaper up north."

He smiled. "I suppose I wasn't really cut out to be a journalist. I wanted to choose the stories I covered, the causes I espoused. On a big city newspaper you're supposed to do as you're told and sometimes there's a fine line between publicity for the public good and exploitation of victims who've already suffered enough."

"So you've freelanced instead. Don't you ever worry that you won't sell a piece and you and Meggie will have to go hungry?" So far, he had scrupulously paid half of the expenses, but Alex privately worried that he was running out of money, since he never mentioned being paid for an article.

"Nope, I never do," he replied, closing the refrigerator door and turning to open his arms to her. "I worry more about not getting enough hugs."

Nestled against his chest, Alex closed her eyes and enjoyed the physical closeness, while worrying a little about a certain emotional intimacy that seemed to be lacking. They never discussed the past, or the future beyond the end of the month. He never told her what he worked on all the hours he spent at his typewriter. When she asked a question she received an answer that left her unsatisfied. Portrait of a man who doesn't want to be tied down, she told herself, and vowed to cure herself of being addicted to him.

His finger went under her chin to tip her face upward so that he could kiss her. As his tongue explored her mouth his hands slipped to the front of her blouse and he began to unbutton it. She wanted to say, stop, I need to talk and I can't when your mouth and hands and body make me forget all reason.

But it was too late, he was already weaving his magic, bringing a response from her flesh that she was sure had nothing to do with the conscious wish of her mind.

The familiar thrill of anticipation coursed along her veins and sensory nerves sent urgent messages of need to that central core of her being that Will O'Keefe alone seemed to command. She sighed and opened herself to him completely.

"Such a long day without you," Will murmured against her mouth as first her blouse and then her bra drifted to the floor. Her breasts were warm, softly pliant yet with tiny rigid peaks that pressed invitingly against his hands. Caressing her, he was struck again with her sheer silken beauty, and the perfection of her slender body that was so surprisingly strong and resilient.

The first time he made love to her he had been so afraid of hurting her. Acutely aware of his greater physical size and strength, he had held back, tried to tether his blinding need and the force of his drive.

But as the days and nights drifted by they had learned each other's needs and desires, the rhythms and nuances, the art of giving, the knowledge of when to demand. Alex was so responsive to his touch, and he to hers, that he no longer exercised that control over his passion. There were times for leisurely teasing, stroking, playfulness, and times, like tonight, when he couldn't wait to possess her.

Stopping only to step out of his swim trunks, he bent her backward toward the couch and they had joined even before her head touched the pillow. Her hair came loose and her arms encircled him as she whispered, "Will, oh, Will . . . yes."

His senses were filled with her, the sight and scent of her and the wonderful murmuring sounds that came breathlessly from her lips. Her slender hips undulated under him, drawing him deeper into a moist heat that swirled about him as they flew together toward that miraculous moment when there would be no time or space or anything in the entire universe but the sensation of ultimate physical joy.

Yet even as they made their way toward that zenith, their ragged breaths and wild rhythms out of control, Will heard the distant warning voice repeating . . . body and mind and soul, how can we separate them?

They were falling back to earth. Clutching one another as they descended, panting and whispering words of love, enclosed in each other's arms, whirling in a ballet of sensuality that had the power of healing within it. Together like this, could anything, anyone, ever drive them apart?

When they lay peacefully, Alex's fingers making small circles on his chest, his hand tangled in her hair, he resolutely shut out the doubts he had about their future. If they were not voiced, perhaps they would cease to exist.

"Funny," Alex said with a hint of a giggle in her voice, "I was hungry when I came home. Now, I suddenly feel quite satiated."

"Nevertheless, you have to keep up your strength to wrestle Great Danes and Bull Mastiffs. Stay here and I'll fix dinner. I caught a bonita this morning. We'll have it with hot tortillas and salsa."

She lay back and stretched her arms languorously over her head as he uncoiled himself and went into the kitchen. She supposed she should go and shower, but for the moment just wanted to luxuriate in her sense of contentment.

Will came back with the folded copy of the *Sand Point Bulletin* which he'd fished out of the grocery bag. "Here, something to keep you quiet while I cook. You can find out who's doing what to whom."

A moment later she was on her feet and standing at the kitchen door. "Will, I guess I'm really in trouble now."

He looked up from the task of boning the fish. "What happened?"

"A new veterinary surgeon is opening a clinic and pet hotel in town. There's a story about him in the *Bulletin*."

"And the town isn't big enough to support two of you," Will said slowly. "You think the Barringtons invited him here?"

"The news item says he has a contract to take care of the Barrington horses. That used to be a big part of my practice. He'll also get all of the small animals belonging to the Barringtons' friends. Apparently he's building a deluxe pet hotel so he'll probably get all the boarded pets when their owners go away on vacation."

"Leaving you with Frances and Ambrose and a handful of dogs and cats belonging to their friends and a barter system for taking care of the *barrio* animals," Will commented. "I'm sorry, Alex. This is all my fault."

She moved swiftly to his side, put her arms around him and held him closely. "I'm not sorry. Some things come with just too high a price. Even if you hadn't come along, I doubt I would have gone on paying it indefinitely."

His dark eyes locked with hers and for an instant all she hoped for and longed for was written in the depths of his gaze. Then he seemed to wrench all of his emotions back from her, leaving her bewildered, but too proud to question him. She said lightly, "How long before we eat? The prospect of another round with the Barringtons has whetted my appetite."

11

The new veterinary surgeon, a Doctor Darrell Derby, paid a brief professional courtesy call on Alex. He was young, earnest and dressed in a three-piece suit. He assured her, without quite meeting her eyes, that his practice would not infringe upon hers.

"No, I guess it won't," Alex said. "Nowadays my patients are mostly elderly poodles from Nob Hill, or tomcats with bitten ears from the *barrio.*"

The sarcasm was apparently lost on him. He expressed the hope that she'd have a nice day, and departed. She knew that he was living at the Barrington estate, taking care of their horses and hounds as well as the Shar-pei. His small animal practice was conducted from an office two blocks down the street from her pet hospital until his new deluxe pet hotel was completed.

Since that particular morning she had only one appointment which wasn't for another hour, Alex went back to cleaning the now empty dog runs behind the pet hospital.

"Now that ain't no proper work for a lady doc," a gruff voice announced.

Cosmo leaned against the chain-link fence that separated the runs from the rear alley. As usual, he wore a fisherman's pullover and his jeans were tucked into rubber boots. But there was a new and surprising addition to his attire. Slung over one shoulder was an expensive-looking leather camera case.

"Good morning, Cosmo," Alex said. "I've nothing better to do, to tell you the truth."

Cosmo rattled the locked gate. "Let me in, Doc."

Alex did so. She felt the need of someone to talk to. The visit of the rival veterinarian had begun to take on the aspects of the prison padre's last call on the condemned man. The Barringtons didn't need to try to break her lease on the pet hospital, the advertisements for the new pet hotel would effectively kill what was left of her business. There would be wall-to-wall carpets in the "suites," a team of dieticians to provide gourmet meals for pampered pets and music piped into each room, which would be fitted with orthopedic beds and individualized toys.

Cosmo carefully hung the camera case on a nail.

"New camera?" Alex asked.

"Uh huh. Used to be a hobby of mine, figured now I'm retired I'd take it up again."

He removed the rake from her hand and motioned for her to go and sit on the bench near the rear door.

"You really don't have to do that, Cosmo."

"Now, now. You was the only one in this town who was kind to an old man. I don't forget that easily. 'Sides, I've a favor to ask of you, Doc."

"Of course, anything."

"I knowed I shoulda kept out of town, after that last warning I got. But, well my friend asked me to come in, and I couldn't refuse."

"Oh, no, not your car again?" Alex knew that he'd been stopped several times and warned about a noisy muffler, broken taillights and a possibly defective smog device.

He nodded sheepishly. "This time I parked in a no-park zone and they done towed it away."

Alex stood up immediately. "I'll drive you over to get it. They keep impounded cars in a lot outside of town."

"No ma'am, not now. I've a few things to do around town first. Thought maybe when you closed up tonight?"

"Yes, I'll be glad to. Just come back when you're finished with your business."

She watched him for a moment, thinking about his visits to town. He always stopped in to see her and always inquired about Frances and Ambrose and the Munro sisters. Alex had resisted the urge to ask about his interest in them, but her curiosity was getting the better of her.

"You haven't asked about the Misses Munro," she said.

His faded eyes gave her a startled glance, before he resumed raking the dirt. "No . . ."

"Frances and Ambrose once belonged to you, didn't they, Cosmo?"

He drew a deep breath. "Not exactly, no."

"What kind of answer is that?"

"Well . . . I did *know* them two critters before they went to live with the Munro ladies. But they weren't mine, no ma'am."

"Then whose were they?"

"Well, I'm not at liberty to say."

Inside the building the telephone rang shrilly and Alex went to answer it, her curiosity far from satisfied.

Doctor Derby was on the line. "Dr. Aimes? I quite forgot the main reason I came to see you today. I need the health records of some of your former patients. No rush on most of them, but I would like the Barringtons' record on their Shar-pei, as soon as possible. Could I send a messenger over today?"

"Of course," Alex said coolly, irritated that he hadn't had the courage to ask her in person. "But if Mrs. Barrington claims there's some emergency, I can tell you right now that the only thing wrong with Star of the East is that he's overfed and under-exercised."

When she went back outside, Cosmo and his new camera were gone. He called later that afternoon to tell her he wouldn't need a ride to the impound yard, he'd already retrieved his car.

Alex lay beside Will on the still-warm sand, watching the day fade into evening. Usually she loved these last moments before darkness claimed the earth, but this evening a special poignancy wafted in with the twilight.

They had swum and played in the surf, laughed and talked of everything but what was on their minds. Tomorrow the beach cottage would no longer be theirs. All of their possessions had been removed to either the storeroom at the pet hospital or to Will's boat. Packing the last of her books that day, Alex had felt as though her whole life was coming to an end. How quickly disaster could creep into the most orderly of lives.

"Don't be sad," Will said, rolling over on to his side and propping himself on one elbow. With his other hand he stroked her bare shoulder. "I'll try to be as good a landlord as you were."

"It isn't that," Alex said. "I feel . . ."

"That you're slipping backward, that you're losing yourself as well as all you've worked and studied for. You're a little apprehensive about what might happen next."

"Something like that, I suppose."

"Not something *like* that. Tell me, are you sorry you took a stand against the Barringtons?"

She sighed. "Sometimes I can't believe anything I've done these past weeks."

He bent and kissed her lips, leaving a pleasantly salty imprint behind. "I like to think I freed you from a fate worse than. . . . But sometimes I'm not so sure you wouldn't have been happier if I hadn't meddled in your life."

"Everything I did, I did of my own choice," Alex responded, sitting up abruptly. "What colossal male ego to believe that you changed my life."

"You changed mine," Will said softly.

"Oh? I wouldn't know about that, since you never talk to me about your life. We just seem to skirt around the edges of it."

"You want a pedigree," Will said drily, "and you're angry because I refuse to supply one."

"That's not fair."

"No? You made it fairly clear that my lifestyle bothered you, not to mention my apparent lack of education, of possessions, of roots. I guess I've been hanging around waiting to find out what it is you do like about me."

Physical things? Alex asked herself silently. Your body, the way we make love, the way we laugh and play together? No, more than that—your companionship, your quiet strength, your refusal to compromise about anything. And the one article of yours I've read impressed me with both its clarity and its compassion. If you lack formal education, Will O'Keefe, then somehow you obtained a knowledge of both the world and people and language that is beyond most people's grasp. If I were to tell you these things, she wondered, how would you react? More importantly, how vulnerable would that admission leave me?

"While you're debating with yourself whether or not to answer my question," Will said, "let me tell you that although you're a very attractive woman, I've never particularly cared for hard-driving career women with set-in-cement standards and expectations. I probably would have walked right on by except for seeing that fatuous ass Rodney Barrington hanging around you."

"Oh!" Alex said. "Of all the—"

"Go ahead and say it, I deserve it. But let me add that after I got to know you, I realized you weren't quite what you seemed. Funny how you can't conceive of the possibility that there might be more to me than meets the eye too."

"You mistook a dedication to my career to blind ambition," Alex commented. "What did you believe me to be, the stereotypical medical practitioner more interested in incorporating and building tax shelters than in healing?"

"Don't put words in my mouth, Alex. I merely meant that I was afraid you'd erected a steel barrier around your heart. Then I realized that the compassion and love you showed to animals extended equally to human beings. But you persist in seeing me as some sort of seagoing bum. Writing for a living has always been suspect, hasn't it? Not a real job someone once said to me."

"Is that what this conversation is all about? Whether or not I accept your lifestyle and profession?"

"Yes. It's important to me to know that you have revised that rather poor first impression of me you formed."

"You're wise and wonderful, Will. I *have* revised that first impression. But it bothers me that you're so secretive about your writing. All I know about it is that you were on the staff of a newspaper and you quit to write magazine articles."

He picked up her hand and blew the sand from her fingers before kissing her palm lightly. "Old habits die hard. I used to be very superstitious about showing anyone my work before it was actually in print. Alex, I wrote a book. It will be published sometime next month. I'm working on a second one."

"Will! How marvelous! Why didn't you tell me before? What kind of a book? A novel?"

"No, no, it's non-fiction. The advance copies should be arriving at the post office in Sand Point any day now. You can read it, if you like."

Alex jumped to her feet, grabbed his hands to urge him

up too. "A celebration is in order. Let's go and open a bottle of wine and drink to the brand-new author."

Smiling, Will stood up. The two dogs, who had been sleeping nearby, suddenly cocked their heads and growled in unison. Will squinted in the direction of the shadowed cottage. "Someone at the door. We'd better go up and see who."

They scrambled up the cliff steps and when they reached the top saw that a sheriff's car was parked in the driveway. A blank-faced young deputy stood at the front door as they came around the side of the cottage.

Will said, "What can we do for you, officer?" Alex grabbed the collars of the two dogs to hold them.

"Mr. William O'Keefe?"

"Yes," Will answered.

"I assume those dogs—the setter and the retriever—belong to you and Doctor Aimes?"

"Yes, they do. What's this all about?"

"You recently went to the Barrington estate and made certain threats."

"I went there because my dog was missing. I was angry and said a few things—over the intercom, since I couldn't get inside the gates—that I probably shouldn't have said. What exactly are you getting at?"

"Did you state that if anything happened to your dog, they would be very sorry?"

"I suppose I said something like that. I was frustrated because I thought they knew where she'd been taken and wouldn't tell me."

"Did you threaten that what had happened to your dog might happen to their dog?"

"No, of course not." There was now an edge to Will's voice.

The deputy turned to Alex. "This is just an inquiry, you understand, Doctor Aimes. I don't have a search warrant, but I wonder if you'd mind if I looked around?"

"What are you looking for?" Alex asked.

"The Shar-pei dog called Star of the East that belongs to Congressman Barrington."

12

Alex slammed the Sand Point *Bulletin* angrily onto the counter. Through the window of the pet hospital she could see the newspaper office across the street and considered storming over there to let them know what she thought of their yellow journalism.

The big story in town was, of course, the so-called dognapping of the Barringtons' expensive Shar-pei. The *Bulletin* carried a thinly-veiled editorial about motives of revenge, and all but tried and condemned Will O'Keefe in print.

Despite the absurdity of the accusation, Alex found herself to be judged guilty by association. Now the entire town was against her. She'd had no patients for the past two days, ever since Star of the East disappeared.

The attitude in town was that while it was one thing for an outsider to challenge the Barringtons on such matters.

as legislation to prohibit backyard breeding, it was quite another to vent one's frustration and anger on a helpless and trusting animal.

Search parties had been formed to comb the surrounding hills and canyons for the missing dog after a house-to-house search provided no hint as to what might have happened to Star of the East. There had been no ransom demand. Without confiding her fears to Will, Alex worried that if the Shar-pei had indeed run off into the hills, he would fall prey to marauding coyotes, who hunted in packs and had been known to kill domestic cats and dogs.

Will had brought Alex ashore in the dinghy that morning and they'd driven into town together. He'd gone to check at the post office to see if the advance copies of his book had arrived and added, "Maybe afterwards I'll take a quick look around Hidden Canyon, see if there's any sign of the Shar-pei. That's about the only place left that nobody's checked."

"That's a long shot, Will," Alex said. "I think you'd be wasting your time. The only way in is to scale an almost sheer rocky bluff. Star is way too fat and lazy to make a climb like that."

"What if somebody carried him in?"

"Nobody goes to Hidden Canyon, not since a hiker was killed in a fall there some years ago."

"Still, I'd like to go see. I can't settle down to work or do anything else while that damn dog is missing and everybody thinks I did away with him."

"Then let me go with you. Please. I've no appointments. You go to the post office while I take care of Red and Meggie."

They had brought the two dogs to the pet hospital, partly because of cramped living conditions on the boat, and partly because of fears for their safety if there truly were a dognapper in the area. Will had reluctantly agreed to return for her before setting off for Hidden Canyon.

From the window she saw him coming down the street. He carried several envelopes, but no package that could have contained a book. As he walked he tore open one of the envelopes, extracted the letter and read it.

By the time he reached the door of the pet hospital, Will's face had broken into a pleased smile and some of the lines of tension had disappeared. Entering the waiting room, he grabbed her and swung her into the air. "Guess what! I just got a letter from my publishers and my book has been awarded a somewhat prestigious literary prize."

"Will! How wonderful! Congratulations. What terrific news. You must be thrilled. I'm so proud of you, I hardly know what to say."

He kissed her and, grinning, added, "That's not all. A television production company is interested in making a documentary, based on my book and they want to option it."

"I'm awed," Alex said, hugging him. "I truly am. But I don't even know what your book is about. You really are the limit, you know."

He looked down at her, several different emotions registering briefly on his face, then said, "The publisher forgot that I asked them to send the advance copies to the Sand Point post office. They're waiting for me . . . somewhere else. Let's go to Hidden Canyon and look for the Shar-pei, then I'll take you on a little journey and tell you about my book."

Alex hesitated, not wanting anything to spoil his day, but she could see that the disappearance of the Barringtons' dog had already clouded everything else for him. No doubt he was remembering how he felt when Meggie was missing and, despite his dislike for the Barringtons, couldn't help but empathize with them. She said, "All right. I've got some hiking boots in the storeroom, I'll get them."

She heard the telephone ring while she was in the storeroom searching through the various boxes containing her personal possessions. Will called, "Alex, it's Miss Munro."

Alex almost tripped over the boxes in her haste to reach the phone. Perhaps everyone in town was not against her, after all.

Miss Munro's precise diction sounded more hesitant than usual as it came over the telephone wire. "Alex? I'm sorry I haven't called you before now. I just read that perfectly dreadful editorial in the *Bulletin,* and I wanted you to know I don't believe a word of it. That nice Mr. O'Keefe couldn't possibly have done such a terrible thing. Oh, I know they don't mention him by name, but it's quite obvious who they mean. When Mr. O'Keefe answered the phone, I told him how my sister and I feel."

"How very sweet of you to call," Alex said. "Thank you."

"While I'm on, I should make an appointment to bring in Frances."

"I saw her very recently, Miss Munro. Unless she has some specific problem, it really isn't necessary to bring her in."

There was a slight pause. "Well . . . I'm afraid she

119

escaped again yesterday. She was rather . . . disheveled when she returned."

"At least she came back voluntarily, I take it? That's a good sign."

"Actually, a gentleman brought her back."

"Cosmo," Alex said at once.

"Yes, he did say his name was Cosmo. How did you know?"

"He's the same man who caught her down at the harbor." Alex glanced up at Will, who was obviously impatient to leave, but she couldn't let the opportunity pass to ask about Cosmo's connection to the Munro pets. "Miss Munro, forgive me for asking, but were you or your sister previously acquainted with Cosmo?"

"Why do you ask?"

"I have reason to believe that Frances once belonged to him. His presence in the area could be the reason Frances keeps trying to escape. She's trying to find her way back to him. Dogs are extremely loyal to their first owners."

"No, no. You're quite wrong, my dear. My sister and I know who used to own Frances and Ambrose. I'm sorry to say their previous owner is deceased."

"And you've never met Cosmo before?"

"Not before yesterday. I believe he's one of those people who have animal magnetism. Frances certainly was already quite attached to him and he to her. In fact he asked if he could take a snapshot of her. I thought it quite touching."

Frances wasn't the most beautiful dog Alex had ever seen, hardly the type of animal to appeal to photographers, amateur or otherwise. A thought struck Alex. "I suppose you had to hold Frances while he took the picture?"

"Why, yes. Otherwise she just wanted to fawn all over him, rolling around at his feet."

Will held up his arm and silently pointed to his wrist watch. Alex nodded, vaguely concerned about Cosmo ingratiating himself with the Munro sisters, but unsure why. She said quickly, "If Frances was out in open country, she might have picked up some fleas or ticks. Would you like to bring her in tomorrow, about nine?"

"Yes, thank you. We'll see you then."

"Now what was that all about?" Will asked as Alex replaced the receiver. "You sounded like you were giving the dear old soul the third degree. Not a proper way to treat your only champion in town."

Alex went back into the storeroom, followed by Will. She said, "I'm not sure. Cosmo knew Frances and Ambrose from somewhere. I suppose I thought he must therefore have also known the Munro sisters, and I was curious about a salty old sea dog's relationship to two rather reclusive and refined maiden ladies. But I was wrong, they just met yesterday. But Cosmo insisted on taking a picture and I have this funny feeling he really wanted a picture of Miss Munro, rather than the dog, as he claimed."

Will glanced at her sharply. "You think he might be setting her up for something, some sort of con game?"

"Oh, no, nothing like that. Frankly, I don't know what I think. I have these jigsaw pieces floating around in my mind that refuse to go together, and won't go away either. Ah, here they are." She pulled her hiking boots from one of the stored boxes.

"Sit down," Will said. "I'll lace them for you. The trick is to lace them tight enough to support your ankles."

Alex perched on a crate while Will kneeled on the floor to ease a boot onto her foot. She commented, "I haven't worn these since my first year in college. Come to think of it, there're a lot of things I haven't done since my first year in college."

Will cradled her ankle in his large strong hands. "Tell me something, what brought you to Sand Point in the first place? You weren't born here, were you?"

She shook her head, remembering. "That little girl, Consuela, who brought in the kitten. Did you know she plays in the alley behind a fancy restaurant all day while her mother works in the kitchen?"

Will's hand tightened slightly around her ankle, a reassuring squeeze that said he understood. Alex went on, "Picture a skinny little towhead in place of a plump dark-haired little girl and you have me. This town was like a bright and shiny page in a picture book to me. I could look at it but never step into it."

Red Baron insinuated himself between them, tail wagging expectantly. She patted the setter's silky head and said, "Sorry, boy, but you're not going with us. You stay here and keep Meggie company."

"I'll take them out to one of the runs, while you find yourself a hat. You're going to need it today. We'd better take a canteen of water too."

He didn't add that the temperature was rising and the chances of a pampered domestic pet surviving without water in the rugged canyons and hills surrounding the town were slim. Still, Star of the East had only been missing a couple of days, perhaps there was still hope.

Alex really hoped, however, that he had indeed been dognapped, and that the culprit would be found.

Alex surveyed with dismay the sheer rocky wall that blocked the entrance to Hidden Canyon. "It's even worse than I'd heard. No wonder no one comes here."

They'd parked her car on the shoulder of a dirt road and walked across the chaparral-covered slopes of the foothills. Alex was already hot and tired. "Will, I'm not sure I can climb that. And I'm quite sure an overweight Shar-pei didn't climb it either. Nor someone carrying one."

He had backed away and, shielding his eyes with his hand, stared at the rock. "There's got to be another way into the canyon."

"There isn't. That's the rock the hiker fell from. People used to fly over the canyon in airplanes and helicopters, trying to find another way in, but nobody ever did. No one comes here any more."

"No? Then how do you account for the fresh tire tracks?"

"Where?"

"Over here." He indicated tracks snaking through the chaparral. "Somebody mustn't have cared about scratching up their car, and been familiar enough with the terrain to know there wasn't any soft sand to get caught in. And that somebody was here within the last few days. We had a light rain shower last week, remember? These tracks were made since then."

He bent to examine the ground more closely, straightened up and began to walk around the hill, away from the sheer rock. Alex called after him, "Where are you going?"

His voice was muffled, as he disappeared into denser brush encircling the hill. "I'm following some footprints— and I believe I just found the way in."

Alex hurried after him, catching up as he reached to pull loose branches away from a rusted sheet of corrugated steel lying against the side of the hill. "What is it?" she asked.

"The entrance to an old mine. Someone carefully covered it up. If it hadn't been for the tire tracks and footprints, it would probably have remained hidden. I've a hunch it leads to something—or someone—who wants to keep the rest of the world out."

Alex shivered. "Had we better go back and—"

"You go back and wait in the car."

"No, Will. Please don't."

He placed his hands on her shoulders and looked down at her. "I don't think anyone would bring a stolen dog here. If it's a ransom situation they're more likely to take the dog to a house somewhere, to be near a phone. There are no phones in this remote canyon. And if the dog was taken to be sold to a laboratory . . . well, again, I just don't think this is the place we'll find the Barringtons' dog."

"Then why go in there?"

"Curiosity. And, I suppose, continuing research. You see, Alex, my book is about displaced and homeless people roaming the country, some through economic necessity, some by their own choice. Men who lost their jobs in the recession, Vietnam veterans who simply dropped out of society. I've come across a number of them living in places like this."

He was researching others of his own ilk, she realized,

perhaps as some sort of justification for his own lifestyle.
"I'll go with you," she said.

"No, you won't. Go on. I'll be back in a few minutes."

Reluctantly she started to walk back to where they'd
left the car, while Will slid the corrugated steel aside and
went into the mine shaft.

She didn't get into the car, feeling it would be uncomfortably hot. Instead she walked around for what seemed
an interminable length of time, until at last she saw Will
emerge from the mine shaft.

When he reached her he said, "There is someone
living in the canyon but I'm quite sure he doesn't have
the Barringtons' dog. He's an elderly man and appears to
be a complete hermit, although somebody has evidently
been bringing him supplies, judging by the tire tracks
and the fact that he told me he never leaves the canyon."

"Does he live in the mine?"

"No, a tunnel comes out inside the canyon and he's
built himself a log cabin there. Did a pretty good job too.
He's made friends with several squirrels and raccoons
and jack rabbits that hang around, which leads me to
believe him when he says he doesn't have a dog."

"How strange, to shut himself away like that."

Will held the car door for her. "Not so strange. I've
interviewed a lot of men like him. Come on, let's leave
him in peace and get back to town. Maybe there's been
some news."

Alex slid into the passenger's seat. "Not so fast. You
promised we'd go and pick up a copy of your book."

"At least tell me what it's called."

"*The Wanderers,* subtitled, A study of the homeless,"

he answered. "After we've checked with the animal control department, we'll go and pick up a copy."

Alex wondered if his reticence to discuss his book had been caused by her attitude toward his lifestyle. Before she had a chance to ask, she was blinded by the sunlight reflecting upon an oncoming windshield.

Will swore under his breath as he swerved to the side of the narrow dirt road, sending up a flurry of dust. The car hurtling toward them seemed oblivious to the fact that the road was too narrow to allow two cars to pass. It came to a halt inches away from their front bumper.

When the dust settled, they looked at the rusting Chevy and its wild-eyed driver. "What in hell are you doing up here?" Cosmo demanded.

Astonished by his unexpected vehemence, Alex burst out, "We were searching for the missing dog. Perhaps you hadn't heard, the Barringtons' Shar-pei is missing."

"I know all about that ridiculous-looking mutt," Cosmo growled. "Looks like a fat monk that somebody folded up and left in a drawer for a month. Took him home yesterday."

"Yesterday!" Will and Alex exclaimed together.

"Last night. Right after I took Frances back to Miz Munro. Them two dogs was running wild all over this hill."

Alex felt the muscles of Will's arm, pressed against hers, contract. His knuckles showed white on the steering wheel. "Dammit, they got the dog back last night, but still let that newspaper editorial hit the streets this morning."

"Perhaps the paper was already printed," Alex suggested, fearing where that rage might lead, in view of the last time he'd confronted the Barringtons.

"They had all night to reset the op-ed page," Will muttered.

"Listen," Cosmo interrupted, his mind obviously on something of more pressing concern to him. "When you was snooping around Hidden Canyon, you find anything?"

"Don't worry," Will answered quickly, "nobody is going to know what we found. You have our word on it."

Cosmo's relief was expressed in a long drawn-out sigh. Will turned the key in the ignition and eased the car around the old Chevy. As they pulled away, Alex asked, "What did we find?"

13

The friend Cosmo has been taking care of, and living with from time to time, until his urge to be on or near the ocean pulls him back. Then he camps out in the caves," Will answered as the car bounced down the dirt road toward the highway.

A misty range of hills separated the inland canyons from the coastal valleys, drawing a jagged line between the harsh high desert climate and the more temperate zone at sea level. Alex could well imagine that a man who had spent a seafaring life would feel claustrophobic and trapped by those mountains, which blocked the view of the ocean.

She said, "He must be very fond of his friend to spend any time with him in Hidden Canyon."

"Yes," Will said. From his expression, even in profile, it was clear that he was thinking about the two men, but he didn't share his thoughts.

"His friend is a very determined hermit," Alex persisted.

"That he is."

"You're identifying with him," she suggested. "In some way I don't understand."

He glanced sideways at her. "You're very perceptive. But forgive me, your car isn't in the best of mechanical condition and we've a fairly high pass to get over. I'd rather concentrate on getting us over the hills in one piece than getting into any heavy discussions right now."

Alex settled back in her seat, feeling shut out.

When they were safely over the pass and beginning the long downward grade toward the coast, she said, "What do you intend to do about the Barringtons?"

"Apart from making sure that they print a retraction? Nothing."

He was still silent and preoccupied when he parked the car off the highway adjacent to the cove where his boat was anchored. Surprised that he'd come directly here, Alex asked, "Aren't we going in to town to pick up the dogs?"

"Not right now. I need to talk to you. Let's walk on the beach, shall we?"

Taking her hand, he led her down a winding cliff trail to the beach. The boat was now anchored off a different cove as they no longer could use the steps at the rear of the cottage. Will had selected this particular cove because it was both sheltered and rarely used by swimmers and surfers due to the dangerous offshore rocks. Alex held her breath when they traveled back and forth in the dinghy during high tides, when ocean swells seemed determined to smash their fragile craft onto the sharp teeth of the rocks.

The sun was still high in the early summer sky and gulls circled overhead, their wings flashing white against a blue sky. Pacific combers rolled majestically toward the beach, the sound of the breaking surf filled the salt-tanged air. Alex glanced at the man beside her as they strolled at the edge of the lapping waves, trying to assess his mood.

So much had happened from the moment his dinghy scraped onto the beach and he stepped into her life, that it seemed in the rush of events perhaps neither of them had had time to step back and examine what was happening.

All at once Alex wasn't sure she wanted a showdown about their relationship, but from the look on Will's face, it was inevitable. Yet he didn't speak, merely squeezed her hand from time to time, and once he stopped and pulled her into his arms and kissed her.

When they reached the point of the bay, he drew her back into the suntraps amid the sheltering rocks. They stood very close, eyes locked, her hands enclosed by his.

He said quietly, "I'm going to have to leave Sand Point soon. A book promotion tour among other things. I don't want to leave you, Alex, but I suppose we both knew we'd only be together for a short time. I'll help you find somewhere to live, of course, and get you moved in. And I wondered if I could leave Meggie with you, at least until her puppies are born."

Feeling an ice-cold hand close around her heart, Alex nodded, not trusting herself to speak.

He said, "Stay here, I'm going for a swim. I need some vigorous exercise and the surf's too dangerous for you today." Turning away from her with a swift movement, he stripped off his faded cotton shirt, discarded shoes and jeans.

She watched, silently, wanting to say, "I love you Will," but that analytic part of her mind stilled her tongue, because what came after that declaration? I'll go with you, throw over my own career just to be at your side? No, that was impossible, and even if it weren't, he still wasn't the right man for her.

More than anything, she wanted to respect and admire Will as much as she loved him. But would that love fade if it were forever faced with a man so totally indifferent to worldly possessions? There was a certain charm to the poverty-stricken writer, starving in his garret or, in Will's case, aboard a weather-beaten boat. But a man who made a commitment to a woman had a responsibility toward a future family too.

She was proud of his accomplishment in writing a book that had won a literary prize, but she knew too that a literary treatise usually brought little in the way of financial reward and that a television option was at best a tenuous link to actual production.

While she admired his humanity and compassion, she wondered if she could accept a man forever clothed in tattered jeans and worn-out tennis shoes. There seemed to be a Peter Pan attitude expressed by his lifestyle that surely wouldn't be such an attractive quality in a few years time. She shivered in the warm sunlight.

The sun was over the sea, and she shaded her eyes with her hand in order to watch as he dived under a wave and came up on the other side, shaking his head. The sunlight found the red glints in his hair and his broad muscled shoulders gleamed bronze against the aquamarine surface of the sea. With powerful strokes, he swam with the approaching wave until it picked him up and for a split second he was outlined against the translucent tunnel of water, perfectly formed, a sleekly wonderful specimen of a man.

She was aghast at her feelings. Here was a man who had won a literary prize and she saw him as some sort of magnificent animal without intellect. Then she realized that the reason for that was his refusal to offer his mind to her, as he'd offered his body. She was overwhelmed with sadness, blinking away a tear as she whispered, "All right, Will. I'll let you go without a struggle. We're not right together."

He rode the wave to the shallows, stood up, the water glistening on his naked body, and walked toward her. Before he reached her she was already sliding out of her own clothes in a fever of need. If this is to be our last time together, then I want him, oh, so desperately.

She lay back on the warm sand and he towered over her, shedding droplets of saltwater that both stung and stimulated her bare skin. Looking down at her, she saw passion ignite in his eyes, and didn't look for love there. She wanted only physical release from the turmoil of her body. She didn't want to think, simply to feel.

He dropped down beside her, his mouth closing over hers in a hungry kiss that sent a shudder rippling through his body. Alex clutched his back, pulled him over until he was lying on top of her, oblivious of his weight, wanting only to be a part of him.

His desire was several paces behind hers, and he tantalized her with slow, loving kisses, with hands that caressed gently, ignoring her fevered responses.

Her torment was exquisite. She was so finely tuned she felt like a bowstring drawn so tightly it must break under the strain. Her body moved under his, inviting, demanding; yet still he held back, his lips moving from her mouth to trail lightly down her throat, burying themselves in the hollow of her neck.

Seizing his head, she forced him back to her mouth and tried to convey her urgency with her tongue and teeth and lips. When it seemed she could no longer bear the suspense, he slid between her thighs and entered her.

Wrapping arms and legs about him, she rose to meet his slowly building thrusts, glorying in him, in herself, in the magic they created together. Beneath her the sand gently grazed her bare back, the sunlight played on her closed eyelids, and she smelled the sea and the clean masculine scent of Will. All of her senses were engaged, all of her lost in this moment.

They crashed over the edge of the abyss together and as they fell to earth, Will whispered her name, over and over again, and she thought perhaps in that murmured incantation she could hear her own sadness and despair that the future wasn't to be theirs.

She felt his hands, large and strong, clasp her face and bring her toward him. "Open your eyes, Alex. Look at me."

Her eyelids fluttered upward. The blazing honesty in his eyes unnerved her. "Will . . ." she began weakly.

"No need to make any pat speeches. We both know it's going to be tough, but better now while we've both got places to go and things to do. My main regret is that I'm leaving you here—you don't belong with all this insulated wealth, Alex. I wish I could persuade you it's time to move on and build a practice somewhere else."

"Let's not start with that old refrain again." She wriggled free of his embrace, suddenly aware of her nakedness, of the sand under her and the sun still high in the sky. Fumbling with her clothes, she said, "This isn't me. I feel bewitched."

"And you credit me with that? This is you, Alex, the real you. That oh-so-professional woman I met was only one facet of your personality."

She reflected silently that she was grateful for that. The free spirits of the world left a lot of misery in their wake. Aloud, she said, "You know, my mother married someone like you. She spent the few years they were together wondering where her next meal was coming from until my father decided a wife and baby slowed him down."

A veil, or perhaps an armored shield, descended over his face. "Ah, I begin to see."

"No, you don't. There isn't a man alive who knows how a woman feels about putting roots down, having security—"

"There's no such thing as security, Alex, believe me. It's an illusion."

Incredulously, she saw that a small smile hovered about his mouth, as though he'd got what he wanted from her. He picked up his tattered, salt-caked jeans and put them on.

Alex moved into a large complex of tiny identical apartments in a beach community twenty miles up the coast from Sand Point. Since pets weren't allowed, she was forced to keep Red Baron and Meggie at the pet hospital, where, sharing the same quarters, they at least had each other for company.

She found herself putting in long hours at the hospital rather than facing going home to the depressing and sterile emptiness of her apartment. At the hospital she at least had Red and Meggie to talk to, along with a steadily increasing trickle of former clients who evidently had decided to defy the Barringtons and return to her.

Will had left her a copy of his book, *The Wanderers,* before he sailed away one evening. She read it in a single sitting, staying up all night to finish it.

The book was an insightful study of the new breeds of homeless wanderers and dropouts from society, from the derelicts of Skid Row, to the ranks of unemployed high-tech engineers or academics who could no longer maintain expensive households and simply gave up, to the "bush vets" of Vietnam with psychological reasons for becoming recluses.

Will's prose had a compelling immediacy and his imagery was lyrical. Rather than merely giving profiles of the people he'd interviewed and studied, or "telling" about their lives, he had written his book in the form of a novel, allowing the people he wrote about to demonstrate their own stories, breathing life into his characters and drama into his scenes.

Nor was the book depressing. Although there were sad stories that made Alex weep, there was also wry humor, and people on those pages who loved their freewheeling existence. It was those happy wanderers that made Alex realize that in describing them, Will had also described himself. He simply marched to a different drummer, as they did. No one could have been so perceptive and insightful as he, without belonging to that select group of individuals. His was a story written from the inside.

She realized now why he had been reluctant to discuss his book, or his writing, or his own lifestyle. Leaving a copy of the book with her to read after his departure was not only his way of saying goodbye, it was also a way of explaining why their brief love affair had been simply an interlude, for both of them right from the start.

Even so, the first stage of her loss of Will tore her heart to shreds and, had she known where he was, she would have dropped everything to go after him. She wanted to hold him and say, "Nothing else matters but you. I can't live without you."

But she received only a postcard from New York, inquiring solicitously about his dog and wishing her his "best." There was no return address.

This brought on the second stage of her grief—anger. How could he do this to her? Walk into her life and disrupt it completely, then simply walk out again without a backward glance.

Meggie's presence was a constant reminder of Will, and Alex regretted agreeing to keep the retriever. Because she needed exercise, as did Red Baron, Alex would load both dogs into her car and drive to the isolated cove where Will's boat had been anchored.

Walking on the beach brought back more memories of Will. She knew it was the worst thing she could do, but did it anyway, and when her face was wet with tears she pretended it was only sea spray. The two dogs, sensing her pain, would rub their silky hides against her bare legs, nuzzle her gently and look at her with sad brown eyes.

"You miss him too, don't you?" she asked, stroking their heads. One evening just before sunset a sailboat came into view and for a moment her heart skipped. But it wasn't a battered sloop. It wasn't Will's boat.

A postcard arrived from him about once a week, always from a different place. He was either on a book promotion tour or was back to his old wandering ways, she didn't know which, and tried to tell herself she didn't care. He was a drifter. He enjoyed that life; she never could, so what was the use of torturing herself, of missing him so much she couldn't think about anything else?

Her practice limped along, then, surprisingly, began to pick up again. Former patients returned to her, although the deluxe new pet hotel took away all of her former boarders, she found she was again in demand to treat sick and injured domestic pets. At least the small animals. It seemed that the new vet was more a large animal man, specializing in horses and cattle.

Shortly after Will's departure, Rodney Barrington stopped by to see her. She had just finished giving a rabies shot to a nervous Pekingese, and carrying the dog out to the waiting room to return him to his owner, she saw the gold Maserati slide into view.

Rodney greeted her as he came through the door with an affable smile, and then waited politely until the owner of the Pekingese settled his bill and departed.

"How are you, Rodney?" Alex asked.

"Fine, just fine. You?"

"Couldn't be better. Excuse me while I wash my hands, will you?"

He followed her into the examining room and, as she scrubbed her hands, said, "I wondered . . . Well, I've got tickets to a performance at the Globe. I wondered if you'd care to join me next Saturday evening."

Her first instinct was to plead a prior engagement, but some perverse streak in her caused her to first ask, "Tell me, how's the palomino who broke his leg?"

Rodney had the grace to look embarrassed. "I *was* pretty obnoxious that day, wasn't I? Please forgive. I was so enraged at seeing you with O'Keefe. What a relief that he's gone. Well, uh, yes, the palomino is fine. We're keeping him for stud purposes mainly, of course."

"Saturday . . ." Alex said, "I'll have to check my calendar to see if I'm free." She was deliberately slow in drying her hands. "Any word on the proposed legislation to outlaw backyard breeding?"

"As a matter of fact," Rodney answered carefully, "I do believe mother was able to get enough signatures on the petition to put the matter on the next ballot."

"She must be very proud of herself."

"You know, it wasn't my idea to ask you to move out of the cottage. I felt really awful about that."

"Oh, don't give it another thought."

"Can we be friends again, please?"

"I'm not your enemy, Rodney."

"Then will you come to the Globe on Saturday?"

"I can't, I'm sorry. Meggie is getting near her time and I don't want to leave her alone." It was almost true, Meggie wasn't crucially close to delivery, but Alex felt she needed to let Rodney down lightly.

Rodney's expression changed. "That's the dog O'Keefe had. What did he do, go away and abandon her.?"

"No, he didn't. I'm taking care of her until she has her litter."

"Yes, well, we get that legislation passed and there'll be no more of that kind of thing, will there? Probably increase your practice too, since everyone will have to have their animal spayed or neutered."

The telephone rang and Alex grabbed it, glad to have the conversation interrupted. The voice on the other end of the line was unmistakable, but so overlaid with quivering outrage that Alex could scarcely believe she was listening to Miss Munro.

"Alex? Miss Munro here. I'm afraid something dreadful has happened. Could you possibly stop by the house after you're finished at the hospital? I'd rather not discuss the matter over the telephone."

"I'll be there about six," Alex said at once.

A kaleidoscopic collage of images raced around her mind, of the delicately pretty twin maiden ladies, Ambrose the parrot, Frances the scruffy dog . . . and an old sea dog named Cosmo.

14

The Misses Munro received Alex jointly, seated side by side on a pale lavender settee in a window alcove in the drawing room of their mansion. The soft light of late afternoon created twin halos around an identical pair of silver coiffures, while pink ruffled blouses flattered pale complexions.

As their butler showed Alex into the room, she thought again that the sisters must have been stunningly pretty in their youth, and wondered why neither had ever married.

There was also a gray-haired man in the room, occupying an armchair at one side of the fireplace. He arose as Alex appeared.

One of the Misses Munro said, "Hello, Alex, thank you for coming. You know Mr. Moorfield, don't you? He's our attorney. Charles, this is Doctor Aimes, the veterinarian we told you about."

As Charles Moorfield shook her hand, Alex felt her curiosity change to apprehension. Attorney? Some sort of lawsuit? Surely not a malpractice suit against her! But what had she done? She'd taken care of Ambrose the parrot and Frances the dog, and both were in good health the last time she saw them.

Apparently sensing her apprehension, Miss Munro— Alex never knew which one was which—said at once, "We asked Charles to be here today just in case we want to take certain legal steps. You see, we think Frances is . . . is *enciente*."

Alex blinked. It was entirely possible—probable— given Frances's many excursions, that she had escaped while she was in heat and had been inseminated. "I'm not sure I understand, Miss Munro. About the legal steps, I mean."

Charles Moorfield, his expression betraying no hint of amusement, answered, "A paternity suit against the owners of the father of Frances's pups. That is, if you confirm our suspicions."

Judging by the tight-lipped faces of the Misses Munro, there was nothing frivolous about their intentions. They were deadly serious. Trying to keep her astonishment under control, Alex said, "Where is Frances? Perhaps I should have a look at her."

One maiden lady rose and crossed the room, opening an adjoining door. "She's in here, Alex. The poor dear is so upset we have Ambrose's cage in here too. I do hope you'll forgive him if he says anything naughty."

Alex closed the door behind her. She was in a glassed-in veranda, filled with plants and ferns, creating a pleasant garden atmosphere for Ambrose's cage and a low leather couch upon which Frances lay.

"Avast, you lubber," Ambrose screamed. "Take off your clothes."

"Oh, hush," Alex said, approaching Frances with outstretched hand. "Hi, Frances, hi girl. How're you doing?"

Frances wagged her tail. Rolling her over gently, Alex ran her hand lightly across the dog's belly, noting the engorged nipples. It was too early to be sure, and probably until any pups started to develop, even an X-ray wouldn't confirm the Munro's suspicions. But, judging by her teats, it was a distinct possibility.

Alex fondled the dog's ears, wondering what she should say to the sisters and their attorney. *A paternity suit?* The whole idea was, of course, ludicrous.

Her first thought was that she wished Will were here to share this with her, but then, so many things that happened gave her that feeling. Still, in this particular instance, he would surely get a charge out of the situation especially in view of Meggie's "marriage by nature" with Red Baron.

Another thought occurred to her. In the case of Meggie and Red, there was little doubt who the father was, but how could the Munro sisters possibly know who had fathered Frances's pups?

"Kiss me, baby," Ambrose cackled. He jumped up and down on his perch and added several four-letter words.

"You're a bad boy, Ambrose," Alex said, grinning. She patted Frances and walked back toward the door.

"Bad boy, bad boy," Ambrose screamed as she went back into the drawing room.

Three pairs of eyes observed her expectantly. Alex cleared her throat. "It's much too early to tell. We'll have to wait for any possible litter to begin to develop. However, if you're concerned, and don't want Frances to have pups, I could perform a hysterectomy now which would—"

"Absolutely not!" The Misses Munro exclaimed in unison. "We *hope* Frances is going to have puppies."

"You do? Then what's all this about a paternity suit?"

Identical smiles curved the sisters' pale pink lips. "Do you remember what that nice Mr. O'Keefe said in regard to the Barringtons' wanting to pass legislation to prevent any breeding outside of the recognized kennels?"

"I do indeed," Alex answered. "He practically called Amelia Barrington a female version of Hitler."

One Miss Munro rose dramatically to her feet to make her announcement. "The paternity suit will be brought against the Barringtons' Shar-pei. Star of the East is the father of Frances's puppies."

"My Dad says it's a lot of nonsense," the little boy said as Alex weighed his terrier puppy. "He says it's a pity some people don't have better things to do."

"Your dad's a judge, isn't he? Small Claims court, as I recall," Alex commented.

"Uh huh. He said it's a waste of time for the Misses Munro to sue Mrs. Barrington."

"That's what he said, did he?" Alex inserted the needle carefully into the terrier. "There, now we'll get him a tag that says he's had his rabies shot and you'll be all set."

"Doctor Aimes, what's a paternity suit?" The little boy asked worriedly. "I know it has something to do with dogs. Will my Muffin get sued?"

Alex smothered her smile. "Oh, I don't think you need worry about it. At least not for a while."

She was about to try to explain, in a general way, what "paternity suit" meant when she heard Red Baron begin to bark. There was an excited urgency to his barking that demanded attention. The setter wasn't usually a barker and, fearing that someone was bothering the dogs out back in the runs, Alex handed Muffin back to his owner.

"I've got to run. Just keep him quiet for the rest of the day, okay?"

If Red Baron had been a human male, he would have been pacing nervously around a maternity hospital waiting room, a box of cigars in his hand. As it was, the setter, making whimpering sounds of sympathy, circled Meggie, who lay on her bed panting, her body twisting and straining convulsively.

Alex went to her and stroked her head. "Good girl. It's all right, Meggie, I'm here. You're going to be just fine. You hang in there while I get the anxious father out of here."

Holding Will's book in her hand, Alex looked at the jacket photograph as she cradled the phone against her shoulder waiting for the receptionist to come back on the line. Will's face regarded her with an eager smile, questing eyes asking some unspoken question.

The black-and-white picture didn't do him justice, since his tanned skin and the red-gold glints in his sandy hair were missing, but some of his vitality and zest were there. The thrust of the shoulders, the muscles bulging under the inevitably ancient cotton shirt. His hair was slightly untidy, as though he'd merely run his hands through it before stepping in front of the camera. But then, that was Will. Why did she want to change him when she loved him just the way he was.

Damn, she thought, why do I allow myself to even think like that?

The publishers' receptionist came back on the line. "According to his itinerary, he should be in Chicago today. He has a TV talk show to do and a couple of radio interviews. I can give you the number of the Chicago television station if it's an emergency."

"Well, it's not exactly an emergency," Alex said slowly. "But perhaps—if you need to talk to him about anything else, that is, you could tell him he just became honorary grandfather to five red-gold pups. Mother, three sons and two daughters all doing fine. And the proud father is almost impossible to be around."

The woman on the other end of the line laughed delightedly. "His Meggie had her litter. I'll call him right away. He's been so worried about her."

But not worried about me, Alex thought dejectedly as she hung up the phone. He hasn't even called. Just a few rotten postcards. In all fairness, he had told her to contact his publisher for the promotion tour itinerary if she needed to talk to him, and she also had his literary agent's number. But why hadn't he called her?

She went back to the room that housed Meggie and her puppies. Red Baron was pressed to the wire partition separating his sleeping quarters from hers, a precaution against his exuberance around the newborns.

Alex looked at the fluffy bundles nestled against Meggie's body. Even now, at only a few hours old, it was evident that they would be beautiful dogs, inheriting all of the best features of both the setter and the retriever.

"You must be very proud, Meggie, and Will is going to love your family."

It had been a difficult delivery, two of the pups having been breech births, and Alex had decided to spend the night at the pet hospital to keep an eye on Meggie.

Exhausted from a long and hard day, Alex slipped off her surgical gown, locked the front door, and went to the neighboring cafe. She ordered a hamburger and pot of tea and sat at one of the sidewalk tables, although a stiff breeze had sprung up and the evening was cool.

There were several other couples at the outdoor tables. They leaned close together, heads almost touching, and spoke in soft tones. Hands reached across tables and clasped. There was conversation and laughter, the sharing of thoughts and ideas and all the little events that make up a day. Alex envied them in a way she had never before envied anyone. The world is full of couples, she thought, and I'm alone.

Why had loneliness never been a problem before she met Will? What you've never had, you never miss, a distant voice whispered. Well dammit, she'd adjust, eventually.

The food had no taste. She choked down a greasy mouthful and gave up.

Back at the pet hospital, she dragged the couch from the waiting room back to the area in front of the delivery room where Meggie and her pups were. Releasing Red Baron from his quarters, she dropped to the couch, the setter curled up at her feet, and slept.

Awakening suddenly, it took her a moment to remember where she was. Red Baron was barking furiously and someone was ringing the front door bell.

She stumbled to the light switch, flipped it on, and went into the waiting room. The outline of the man on the frosted glass of the door was unmistakable. Flinging it open, she almost collapsed into Will's arms. For some utterly unknown reason, the instant she felt those strong arms around her, she began to cry softly, pent-up tears she hadn't even known were waiting to come out.

15

Will held her as she mumbled against his sodden shirt front, "I'm sorry, I don't know why I'm doing this. I never cry."

"It's okay, Alex, this is me, Will. With me you can do whatever you want to do."

As her sobs subsided, he slipped his arm around her and led her into the waiting room, closing the door to the street.

Feeling suddenly foolish in the bright white overhead light, she brushed her fist across her eyes. "I had a hard day," she said defensively, "and you scared me, arriving in the middle of the night. I was sound asleep."

"I did call your apartment from the airport and went straight over there when we landed. I waited around for a while and then it occurred to me you must be here. I tried to call, but you must have been dead to the world. It's not exactly the middle of the night either, look."

He opened the Venetian blinds on the window and Alex could see a silver dawn gilding the hills on the far side of the bay. There was an intense clarity to the sky, no hint of cloud or sea mist, and a certain sharpness in the early morning air that registered vaguely on her sluggish consciousness.

"I must have been tired if I didn't hear the phone." She looked at him, seeing that there were tired lines etched into his face too. "Oh, I'm sorry. You want to see Meggie, of course. Come on."

He caught her by the arm as she turned away, and pulled her back. "Is everything all right?"

"Yes, Meggie's fine and the pups are beautiful. I just wanted to keep an eye on them last night. Besides, by the time she delivered it was quite late and as you know I have a long drive to my apartment. It was easier to spend the night here."

"I didn't mean was Meggie all right; I have enough confidence in you to know she was. I mean, is Alex all right? I've never seen you cry before."

"I'm fine. I don't know what made me do that. Perhaps it was something left over from a sad dream."

He gave a ghost of a grin. "For one mad moment I even hoped that you'd missed me as much as I missed you."

But not enough to take a minute to call me, she thought, as she came fully awake and her rational mind took over. "Come and see Meggie. She really missed you."

She led the way back to Meggie's room, Red Baron prancing in front of them, tail feathers swishing back and forth in a flurry of proud anticipation. Alex stood in the doorway as Will went to his dog's side and bent over her.

The lump came back to Alex's throat as Will tenderly petted Meggie then gently picked up each puppy in turn. Meggie's tail thumped weakly and she gazed at Will adoringly. He was so sensitive, so caring, that— unreasonably—Alex wanted some of that caring to be directed her way. Yet when had she ever given him a word of encouragement? She had simply kept on agreeing that they were wrong for each other, despite the fact that when they were together everything they did took on a wonderful golden glow. And when they made love . . .

Will looked over his shoulder at her. "In your message to my publisher about my honorary grandfather status— which broke them up, by the way—you didn't say anything about your honorary grandmother part in this. Must say that you're the youngest, best-looking grandmother I ever did see."

"We'll have no trouble finding homes for the pups," Alex said, more out of need to say something that would divert his and her own attention from the fact that she was feeling very emotional. Why, she wasn't sure. Will was back and she was acting as if he were leaving her. Perhaps that was it—the fact that he *would* leave again and she wasn't sure she could stand it.

"They're cute little guys, aren't they?" Will answered with a fond smile, scratching a tiny ear. "I'm not sure I want to have them adopted."

"Well, you certainly can't keep six dogs aboard your boat," Alex pointed out. "Where is your boat, by the way?"

"Moored at a dock up in Dana Point. I left her there when I went to New York." He straightened up. "I don't know about you, but becoming a grandfather has given me an appetite. How about some breakfast?"

"Sounds like a plan. I didn't have much time to eat yesterday. I'll just get fresh water for the dogs."

Fifteen minutes later they went to the only coffee shop open at five in the morning, slid into a booth and ordered the breakfast special from a waitress who was still half asleep.

Leaning back against bright orange plastic, Will watched Alex with a small smile playing about his mouth. She noticed for the first time that although as usual he wore no jacket, he was wearing a very nice shirt—with a small damp patch on the front—and well-tailored slacks. There was even, surprise of surprises, a tie knotted loosely at his throat. Despite a night flight from Chicago and subsequent drive from the airport, he managed to look like a well-to-do business executive who'd just shed his jacket.

She glanced down at her own crumpled blouse—with a small stain on the sleeve—and badly creased skirt. Her hair, fastened in a knot on top of her head, must resemble a rat's nest, with escaping tendrils and loose pins. She knew without looking that she must have pressed more creases into her cheek, from sleeping without a pillow on the rough surface of the couch. And, of course, to top it all off, her eyes would be red from crying. What a sight she must be!

"You look like hell," Will said cheerfully, as though reading her thoughts. "Funny thing is, you look the way I did, before I left."

"Thanks. That's just what I needed to hear."

"Sorry about that, but it *is* just what I needed to see. You've no idea how approachable you look this morning."

The waitress placed glasses of orange juice on the table

151

and filled their coffee cups. When she left Alex said, "How is the tour going?"

"I've decided it's much easier to write a book than to promote one. The world seems to be full of interviewers laying in wait for unwary authors, trying to goad them into saying something they shouldn't. Of course, I've seen the other side of the coin, having been a journalist and reporter myself. It's been a rare opportunity for me, studying the situation from both sides. Probably be a good idea if we could apply it to our personal lives, don't you think?"

"Yes," Alex said slowly, "we learn a lot from walking in someone else's moccasins. I believe I know you much better now that I've read your book."

Will leaned forward. "What did you think of it?"

"You certainly know your subject. Although I found myself weeping over some of the sad stories, I finished the book thinking that it's probably *right* for some people to drop out of society and live as free spirits."

"Good. That was my intention. I wanted to step back and look at the subject with an anthropologist's eye."

How could you do that, when you yourself are one of your own subjects? Alex wondered silently. She wasn't going to let the shirt and tie and well-cut slacks fool her. No doubt his publisher had insisted he dress like a successful author for the promotion tour.

"You missed some spicy goings-on here in Sand Point while you were gone," Alex said. She told him about the odyssey of Frances and Star of the East. "Right now we're waiting to find out for sure if she's pregnant. Though the Munro sisters are convinced she is and are acting accordingly."

Will rolled his eyes. "Must be the air in this town—drives hotblooded males crazy, canine as well as human."

"I haven't got to the punch line yet," Alex said. "The Misses Munro plan to bring a paternity suit against the Barringtons."

Will threw back his head and roared with laughter. "You're kidding me!"

"No, I'm not. The Munro attorney has already sent word to the Barringtons. Bart is back in Sacramento, but Amelia is lying low. There's been nothing in the *Bulletin* about it."

"With Frances's wayward ways, how do they know the Shar-pei is the father?"

"Both dogs got out at the same time. Both were found by Cosmo, in an extremely compromising position. He took them both back to their owners. I guess he'll be the chief witness, if the case ever gets to court, but I haven't seen him lately. He hasn't been to town. He's probably staying with his friend in Hidden Canyon."

"You didn't tell anybody about their place there, did you?" Will asked sharply.

"No, of course not. Why do you ask?"

"I gave Anders my word I wouldn't. And my word is very important to me."

"Anders? That's the name of Cosmo's friend?"

"Anders is his first name. It's a Danish form of Andrew I believe. Anders Jensen, an interesting man. If you hadn't been waiting for me that day I'd have stuck around and tried to learn more about him. Gutsy old guy. He'd lost a leg and gets around on a crutch. Told me he has a prosthesis but it's uncomfortable so he doesn't bother with it. Can you imagine finding your way into Hidden Canyon, and building a house there? It'd be hard enough for someone without a handicap."

The waitress placed plates of scrambled eggs and bacon in front of them and, feeling ravenous, Alex fell upon the food. It was only when she finished the last piece of toast it occurred to her that her appetite was always better when she ate with Will.

Will said, "The paternity suit will be tossed out of court, if it ever gets that far. What do the Munro sisters hope to gain by such a crazy scheme?"

"Mainly, I believe, to get the Barringtons to forget about this legislation they want passed to prohibit back-yard breeding. After all, Amelia can hardly espouse it when her own dog fathered mongrel pups."

"In that case, I'm all for it. But they're going to need more than Cosmo's word, don't you think?"

"I'm afraid you're right. But it was a lovely try, wasn't it?" She sipped her coffee and asked, "How long can you stay?"

He sighed. "I promised to do a couple more TV talk shows."

"I'm somewhat ashamed to say I haven't seen any of the ones you've done. Not that I've had much time to watch TV lately, but—"

"They've mostly been on local channels, PBS and so on. No prime-time stuff. Look, Alex, I want to settle up what I owe you for taking care of Meggie, and I'd appreciate your boarding her and the pups for another few weeks, until they're old enough to move. And I want a bill that would be the same amount you'd charge for your services to any resident of this town, okay? No special deals."

"I'll make up a statement for you when we get back to the office," Alex said dully. Why didn't he say something on a personal level? She was ready to scream with frustration.

"You're not offended are you?" Will asked.

"No. I'm not a charitable organization. I expect to be paid for my services." She resolutely shoved aside the thought that the bill would be considerable, adding boarding, food, etcetera and might be out of reach of his limited budget.

"Good. But no need to bother with a statement. I'll write you a check and you can fill in the amount later."

She watched as he pulled a checkbook from his pocket and wrote the check. There seemed to be a finality about the act that brought back her feeling of despair. He's moving out of my life, forever, and I can't stand the pain.

Her smile was cool as she accepted the check and shoved it into the pocket of her blouse. "When are you leaving?"

He smiled. "I just got here. I don't have to be at the airport until tomorrow morning. I was hoping we could go out to dinner tonight when you're finished with your work."

A beacon of hope flickered again at the end of a long dark tunnel. "That would be nice." She arranged her knife and fork neatly, side by side on her plate, sat still for a few moments, cool, collected, perfectly composed. Then burst out, "Why the hell didn't you ever call me while you were gone?"

"You didn't ask me to," he answered. "Alex, I don't know what sort of men you're used to, but there are men

155

around who need to know what's expected of them. All of the signals I've been getting from you tell me that I'm only a temporary guest in your life."

It was true, Alex realized. And what made it true was that it couldn't be otherwise for them. Ultimately each had to return to their own world. There was no common ground upon which to meet. Wanting it to exist didn't make it happen.

"Is that the way you see me, as just a temporary visitor?" Will prodded gently.

Her hand lay on the plastic tablecloth and his hand crept toward it and closed around her fingers. "Such small hands for the big job they do. I guess your silence is more eloquent than words."

Every nerve in her body was urging her to deny what he had assumed, to say, no, I don't want you to be temporary, I want you with me forever. But the words didn't come and Will, having patted her fingers in the manner of a father reassuring a troubled child, was now paying the bill and standing up to leave.

Out on the street the sun was already hot, the air so dry it seemed to crackle. The pungent odor of sagebrush wafted in on a strong wind, obliterating the smell of the sea. As the wind whipped Alex's hair across her face and she clutched her billowing skirt, Will put his arm across her shoulder to steady her in the unexpected gust.

"Santa Ana wind," Alex said. "Smell the sage? It's coming down the canyons directly from the deserts. We don't usually get them this early but the weather's been crazy this year. Let's hurry. The desert winds often affect animals the same way they affect humans, makes them anxious, sometimes a little crazy. I guess I know now why I woke up crying this morning."

Will tried to protect her with his own body from the hot dry wind, but it seemed to whirl in every direction, carrying dust and debris that stung her cheeks and got into her eyes. She was glad when at last they slammed the door on the wind.

"Phew!" Will said. "Do they always spring up so quickly?"

"Yes, though there's usually a dryness and a certain stillness in the air that precedes the wind. I suppose I didn't notice it last night."

"It's similar to the Sirocco in Africa, isn't it?"

"The big danger," Alex said as Red Baron came to greet her and complain about her absence, "is fire. We've had no rain to speak of last season and the chaparral in the hills is so dry. One spark and . . ."

She broke off as the door opened again, allowing another blast of hot air to shriek into the room. Cosmo, his face red with windburn, came puffing in. "Blasted wind, like to blow me away. Hi, Doc. Hello Will." Cosmo was clutching a large manilla envelope.

"Hello, Cosmo. What can we do for you today?" Alex asked.

He waved the envelope. "Just got 'em. Didn't want to have 'em developed in town, just in case, you know. The Barringtons could've owned the store."

Placing the envelope on the counter, he began to withdraw several snapshots. "Just stopped by to ask your candid opinion, Doc. I just don't know if I should show these to two refined ladies like the Misses Munro, only they really need 'em as evidence."

157

Looking over his shoulder, Alex saw that Cosmo had snapped several shots of Frances and Star of the East—gamboling together in a meadow, rolling down a hill, nuzzling one another and . . . there was no doubt from the last pictures he took that Frances had mated with the Barrington's Shar-pei.

16

The desert wind was rising in intensity as Will and Alex, accompanied by Cosmo, drove up the hill toward the Munro mansion. Since it was a Saturday, Alex had no appointments at the pet hospital and she'd been lucky enough to find a high school girl to work for her on weekends.

Alex felt almost as buffeted by conflicting emotions as by the increasingly fierce wind. Out of the corner of her eye she could see Will's strongly muscled thighs move under the tailored slacks as he accelerated to avoid a huge tumbleweed bouncing across the road.

She shifted her gaze to his hands on the wheel. Big hands, well-shaped, as though rendered by a sculptor, the fingernails manicured. His fingernails were always immaculate. He was a drifter without roots or personal possessions, but she had to admit that he certainly wasn't of the stereotypical variety. Even when he wore tattered jeans and threadbare shirt, he was always well-groomed, and scrupulously clean.

"Maybe I should wait for you outside," Will suggested as the Munro mansion came into view at the top of the hill. "In view of the fact that Amelia Barrington is going to be there. No point in mixing conflicts. This confrontation belongs to the Munro sisters."

"Now son, Miz Munro invited you to come along. You come on in with us and to hell with Miz Barrington," Cosmo said.

"He's right, Will," Alex put in. "Besides, since the Barringtons hide out behind their electronic fence, it might be your only opportunity to talk to her face to face and tell her to print a retraction in the *Bulletin* for that story they printed accusing you of dognapping Star of the East." Alex knew that Will had gone to the editor of the newspaper before he left on his book tour, demanding that a retraction be printed, but none had been forthcoming.

"Hell, yes," Cosmo agreed. "Always got to fight the dictators of the world, Will."

The car shuddered as a blast of hot wind whipped out of a canyon. Will gripped the steering wheel to keep them on the road. From their vantage point at the crest of the hill they were aware of the vastness of the ocean, incredibly blue as the wind swept the air sparklingly clean. To the east the hills were an ominous brown, the chaparral tinder-dry from lack of rain.

Will turned the car into the driveway of the Munro mansion, passing ornamental wrought-iron gates that were invitingly open, in contrast to the Barrington estate's fortresslike façade.

Amelia's silver Rolls-Royce was parked in front, Herbert, her ancient chauffeur huddled in the driver's seat, waiting for his mistress. Will parked Alex's car behind the Rolls and got out to come around and open her door.

The wind caught them in its dragon breath and Alex clutched Will's arm as they went up the stone steps to the front doors. She had changed into white linen slacks and a cool cotton blouse, tied her hair back with a scarf, and although windblown, felt less scruffy than earlier in the day. Cosmo panted along beside them, cursing the wind under his breath and clutching his envelope of evidence.

They were shown into the library, rather than the drawing room, and Alex assumed this was because the Munro sisters felt this was not exactly a social visit. The library was at the rear of the house, with French doors that opened onto a rear terrace and a view of the hills to the east.

Amelia Barrington sat stiffly on a straight-backed chair near a large relief-type globe of the world. There were also several framed maps of the world on one wall, surrounded by books about the sea and navigation. Noting this, Alex wondered at the interest of two maiden ladies in such a subject, since some of the books looked fairly new and there had been no male Munros around for the past thirty years or so.

The Misses Munro greeted the new arrivals cordially, offered them chairs and indicated a tray upon which stood a frosty pitcher of lemonade, an ice bucket and several glasses.

Amelia said, "This is such a ridiculous waste of time. I certainly wouldn't have dignified such an accusation with so much as an acknowledgment if it had come from anyone else. Miss Munro, I repeat, you've been hood-winked by that disreputable old man and—"

Cosmo thumped the manilla envelope down on the table. "Disreputable, is it? Well now, lady, you just take a look at some pictures this disreputable old man took of your dog."

Alex said, "I'd like to take a look at Frances, Miss Munro."

"Yes, of course. She's in the solarium with Ambrose."

"I know the way," Alex responded. She turned to Will. "Would you like to come too?"

He smiled easily. "No, I'd rather not miss the expression on Mrs. Barrington's face when she sees those pictures."

Alex hesitated, then headed for the door. Cosmo slowly withdrew the snapshots and, with a flourish, spread them across the surface of the table. Amelia's glasses hung from a jeweled chain around her neck and she raised them to her eyes to peer at the pictures.

The Misses Munro, who had already been told that the pictures showed the mating of the Barrington Shar-pei and Frances, averted their eyes.

Amelia's face flushed bright red, her eyes bulging behind her eyeglasses. She opened her mouth to speak, then closed it again. Clearing her throat, she mumbled, "There's gossip in town of a paternity suit. Surely you aren't serious?"

"Oh, but we are very serious," Miss Munro said. The other sister added, "We've already spoken to Mr. Moorfield, our attorney, about the matter."

"There's no need to make such a fuss," Amelia muttered, fumbling with an outsize handbag on her lap. "I'll write you a check to cover your dog's veterinary bills. You can have the litter aborted."

Alex came back into the room and overheard the last

remark. She looked questioningly at the sisters as she said, "I'm pretty sure Frances is going to have pups."

"We certainly will not get rid of Frances's puppies," Miss Munro said. "For one thing, she doesn't belong to us. We're just taking care of her for a friend, and we can't get in touch with him at present."

Cosmo shuffled around the table and went to the window, staring at the dried-out hills with a concentration that indicated he felt his part in the proceedings was over.

"Oh, for heaven's sake," Amelia exclaimed, "Frances isn't a human. You can make the decision to have her spayed without the owner's consent."

Will, who had had a telephone conversation with the sisters before leaving the pet hospital, now leaned forward. "Mrs. Barrington, for once in your life will you please be quiet and listen to someone else? The Misses Munro have something they want to say to you."

"We have certain conditions that must be met," Miss Munro announced. "First, that you drop your ridiculous campaign to outlaw all but kennel-breeding. That all of the money you raised goes to build the animal shelter instead."

Amelia's lips twitched for a moment, as though she found it impossible to agree to anything, least of all the abandonment of her favorite project. Finally she said, "And if I agree, you'll drop the ridiculous lawsuit? You know what a field day the press would have at our expense. It's bad enough that it's already being whispered about here in Sand Point. If the news gets out— you do have this, this reporter person, O'Keefe here—"

"My lips are sealed," Will assured her solemnly. "I'm here only as a friend. However, Cosmo's photographs not only prove that your dog spent some time roaming the hills with Frances, they also clear me of your charge that I dognapped him. Now, I don't give a damn about your allegations, but my good friend Doctor Aimes here lost a lot of business because of the incident. Therefore I feel it's only fair that a complete account of what actually happened is published in your newspaper."

"But . . ." Amelia's face now seemed to twitch all over. "The whole idea is to hush this matter up. If we print the story in the *Bulletin* . . ."

"It's not necessary to go into detail," Will said. "You can simply state that you learned your dog ran loose for a couple of days and you regret any implication that other people were involved in his disappearance. Then you can run a separate story to the effect that you've decided the proposed legislation was ill-advised and that you're concentrating your charitable efforts toward providing the shelter for unwanted pets."

Amelia let out her breath, deflating visibly. "Oh, very well."

The Misses Munro clapped their hands delightedly.

At the window Cosmo suddenly said, "Oh, no! Tell me I don't see what I think I see. 'Cos if I do we've got to get Anders out of there—" He broke off, spinning around to face them, his eyes wide with mortification, whatever he'd seen out of the window forgotten.

Alex, standing near the door, saw the identical expressions of first, shock, then trembling wonder, spread across the porcelain pretty faces of the Munro sisters. They were staring at Cosmo and for an instant those three were the only players in some private little drama.

"*Anders!*" The sisters repeated in unison. "Anders Jensen? He's *here?*"

"Oh, hell," Cosmo said. "Me and my big mouth."

164

One sister looked as if she were about to faint and Alex rushed to her side and helped her to a chair. The other Miss Munro said in a small shaky voice, "So that's why Frances and Ambrose seemed to know you. It was you who left them on our doorstep that night. You're a friend of Anders, aren't you, Cosmo?"

Cosmo shuffled his feet and looked around as though seeking escape. "He wasn't here when I brung them critters to you, ma'am, no ma'am. He was in Hong Kong and he asked me to bring Frances and Ambrose here and leave 'em with you."

The Miss Munro who was more composed than her sister said to Alex, "We found Frances chained to the door knob, and Ambrose in his cage nearby. There was a note fastened to her collar telling us that they had belonged to . . . to an old friend, who was no longer able to care for them and asking if we, for old time's sake, would do so."

"And the old friend was Anders Jensen who is now living in Hidden Canyon," Alex responded, and promptly received hard stares from both Will and Cosmo. "Well, I feel the Misses Munro have a right to know where he is. Why couldn't he have taken his pets back after he returned to this country?"

"Ma'am," Cosmo turned pleadingly to the sisters, "Anders and me was on the same gunboat in the China Seas. We shared a lot of good times and bad times together. And when the war was over we both joined the merchant marine. That's when Anders got Ambrose from a shipmate of his, and later on, after Anders became skipper, he adopted Frances after she stowed away aboard our ship."

"Yes, I understand," Miss Munro said sadly, "but why

did he send us his pets and not let us know he was coming home again, after all these years?"

"Well, ma'am, I'm not at liberty to say."

The Miss Munro who was still standing turned to Alex, "I'm sorry. You don't have any idea what we're all talking about, do you? You see, in our youth, my sister and I used to think it such fun for one of us to date a young man, then the other to accept a date and pretend to be the same sister."

"You both dated Anders Jensen?" Alex asked, beginning to fit the pieces of the puzzle together.

"I'm afraid we both fell in love with him but our parents found him totally unsuitable. He was a young sailor, without education, or background, or . . . breeding, according to our family standards. And when Anders found out the trick we'd played on him— switching dates, both of us going out with him—well, he felt we'd trifled with his affections. He sailed away and we never saw him again. Although we wrote to his ship, he never replied to our letters. My sister and I never quite got over him."

Will said, "So when the dog and parrot appeared, you took them in." He looked at Cosmo. "I think I understand. But, regardless of any promises you made to Anders, these ladies deserve an explanation."

Cosmo said, "Anders was hurt bad. Fell down a shaft aboard ship and mangled his leg. When they took him into that hospital in Hong Kong, they was afraid he'd never walk again. Had to amputate the leg, they did."

The second sister turned pale and sank into a chair next to her twin. They clasped hands and waited for Cosmo to finish his story. "He asked me to bring his pets to you along with that note. I reckon he wanted you to know he'd never forgotten you. He didn't think he was going to make it and even if he did, he thought he'd be paralyzed. Then, next thing I know, after you've already had the critters for a few months, up pops old Anders. Well, he didn't think it was right to take Frances and Ambrose away from you then, on account of he was sure you'd be attached to them.''

Will had wandered over to the window, and now he spoke, his voice sharp with urgency, "Cosmo, I think you're forgetting what caught your attention. And we'd better move if we're going to get Anders out of that canyon in time.''

He was already running from the room when Alex looked out of the window and saw the black plume of smoke rising from the crest of the distant hills. A brush fire whipped by high winds could quickly consume hundreds of acres of dry chaparral and a man on crutches was trapped inside an almost inaccessible canyon.

17

·eeeeeeeeee·

Will drove with reckless abandon toward the column of smoke rising from the hills. At his side Alex tasted the acrid air as they drew closer to the fire, and her eyes stung as she stared at the horizon, trying to estimate which direction the brush fire was moving.

They had left the Misses Munro to call the fire department, and forest rangers. Mrs. Barrington had departed, fearing for the safety of her stable of horses if the conflagration moved down the hillside toward their estate.

Cosmo was in the back seat, and Alex was present by virtue of her medical training. "Look," she'd pointed out when Will tried to argue with her, "my medical bag is in the car. If anybody's hurt, I think I'd be better able to help than you. So shut up and let's go."

They could see the fire now, orange flames licked

along a not-too-distant ridge, moving with terrifying speed through the dry brush.

As they climbed the steep grade leading toward Hidden Canyon, Cosmo leaned forward and said hoarsely, "Look—over to the starboard, more smoke."

Alex rolled down the dusty window of the car in order to have a better view and was instantly aware of the sound of the fire, flames crackling as, wind-driven, they consumed the hillside.

Cosmo was right, a second pillar of smoke was visible, at some distance from the first, but it was possible the two fires could link up somewhere in the vicinity of Hidden Canyon.

No one spoke as Will floored the accelerator and roared toward the dirt road that led to the canyon.

The fire raced down from the north, blackening everything in its path and Alex held her breath as a violent gust of wind dropped glowing embers on the road ahead of them.

They could no longer see the sun, a vast pall of smoke and dust had created a canopy of burnt sienna between hills and sky.

Somewhere behind them they could hear the shriek of sirens as fire trucks approached.

Moments later a borate bomber swept out of the sky, winging over the car at a perilously low altitude. They watched in fascinated awe as the ungainly machine dived sharply and flew between the walls of the canyon, almost grazing the rocks on either side. A red cloud of borate descended on the flames, instantly dousing a wide swath of fire.

"Will you look at that!" Cosmo exclaimed. "That's some kind of flying!"

Alex knew that despite the skill of the pilots, the fire probably couldn't be contained with borate, or water drops. The wind was simply too fierce. A single ember could be whipped into flames again. Usually the fire fighters moved in after the planes, putting out hot spots.

Will turned onto the dirt road and the car bumped over the rutted trail toward the sheer boulders blocking the entrance to Hidden Canyon.

Pulling off the road at the closest point to the mine entrance, Will reached into the back seat and grabbed the length of rope he'd taken from the Munro gardener. "Alex, you stay here. Attract the attention of the first emergency vehicle you see and tell them where we are."

"But—" Alex began.

"Dammit, Alex, I haven't time to argue." Slinging the coil of rope over his shoulder, he ran for the canyon.

Cosmo climbed out of the car and said, "I'm going too. We may need to carry Anders out. He's right, somebody's got to let the firemen know we're in there otherwise they could just decide to let the canyon burn and concentrate on stopping that second fire from jumping the highway."

She told herself they were bigger, stronger, more physically capable of rescuing a handicapped man, and therefore they were right to leave her behind. But oh, how much easier it would be to be doing something, rather than standing on a smoke-shrouded hillside watching the approaching flames.

As the minutes ticked by and the pall of smoke became more dense, she moistened a handkerchief with water from one of the canteens they'd filled, and tied it over her mouth and nose.

170

Unbidden, a horrifying thought formed at the back of her mind. *What if she were never to see Will again?* There was a real possibility that none of the three men would emerge from that fiery caldron.

Her heart began to thump painfully, as though she'd been running hard, and her breath, already rasping in her smoke-dried throat, turned to gasping sobs. She thought, no, no nothing must happen to Will. I love him. I don't want to live without him. How could I have constructed all those stupid obstacles and put them in the way of Will and I being together? All it takes is to be together!

It was so simple, she couldn't believe it, and, lost in the wonder of the revelation, almost didn't realize that the stream of emergency vehicles traveling up the hill were now going right past the turn-off to the dirt road.

She ran back down the road, waving frantically. At the intersection to the highway a sheriff's car swerved over to her. "What happened, your car stall? Come on, hop in, we've got to get you out of here."

"No! No. Please, there are three men in Hidden Canyon. We need help up there."

The young deputy's face registered shock. "*What?* Okay, okay, calm down. Get in, I'll divert the next truck up there."

"I'm not leaving," Alex said, backing off. "Get some help, hurry!" She turned and ran back up the road, the air searing her lungs and the wind whipping her hair.

She heard the deputy shouting for her to come back, that the fire was out of control, but she ran on, heedless of anything but the need to see Will again.

Cutting across the open expanse of chaparral-covered ground between the dirt road and the entrance to the canyon, she blundered into a clump of cholla and felt its spiny needles penetrate her slacks and embed themselves in her skin.

There, just ahead through the pall of smoke, she could see the sheet of corrugated steel and heap of branches that had concealed the mine entrance. The handkerchief over her mouth was bone dry.

Just before she entered the mine shaft she glanced back and saw a fire truck and a rescue vehicle skimming over open country toward her.

The black tunnel closed around her like a tomb and she hesitated, experiencing a wave of claustrophobia. But more than the darkness stopped her progress. The shaft was filled with smoke. She stumbled back outside, coughing and retching.

Arms went around her, supporting her weight, and an indignant voice said, "Lady, what are you trying to do, get yourself killed?"

She wrenched free of the fireman, turning on him in fury. "Will's in there. He's in the canyon and the fire is over the ridge. For God's sake, we've got to get him out."

"Not through that old mine shaft we don't. The smoke'll kill us."

When she tried to run past him, back into the mine, the fireman grabbed her, swung her into his arms and carried her, kicking and struggling, back to where the rescue van was parked.

Alex sobbed, both from fear for Will's safety and because the smoke now whirled in dense black clouds and every breath was agony.

As she was set on her feet, the young firefighter, his face soot-grimed and his eyes red-rimmed, said, "I'm sorry, lady, there's no way we can get into the canyon. The fire's out of control in there."

Overhead the engines of another plane roared, and this time it was a water drop. The water cleared the smoke around the rocky barrier guarding the entrance to the canyon, and, in the seconds before the black cloud again descended, Alex looked up and saw the two figures outlined against the sky.

"Look!" she screamed. "Up there at the top of the boulders."

"Holy cow," the fireman said. "I hope to hell their rope is long enough. Hey you guys, they're going to try to scale that cliff. Get a truck over there and start playing the hose around them but for Christ's sake, don't blow 'em off the rock."

Alex had her fist jammed against her teeth. There'd only been two figures, but she hadn't had much time to look. She ran after the truck and, as the hose sent a fountain of water up the boulder, could see that one man was rappelling—not very skillfully, down the sheer wall of the cliff.

It was Cosmo. The old man landed heavily and winced with pain as the firemen crowded around him. "We need a litter, or a chair, or something, up there. Got a man overcome with smoke. We was going to try to lower him on the rope, then we saw you guys down here."

Alex was never sure how she lived through the nightmare of the next minutes. Of waiting for a rescue chair to be hauled up, then the painstakingly slow descent of Anders Jensen.

The fire was now roaring over their heads, rushing toward that last stretch of barren rock where Will waited,

173

and she knew that the wind would drive the flames over that barrier, and that Will had no protection from them.

She wept without tears, prayed, pleaded to no one in particular to hurry.

Then at last she saw Will rappelling down the rock and, inexplicably, the moment his feet touched the ground, the acrid smoke blacked out her vision completely and she felt herself sway, then slide to the ground. In her last second of consciousness, she thought, why . . . I'm going to faint.

18

Smoke inhalation," a white-coated doctor said to Alex as she opened her eyes. "You'll be all right. Just lie quietly for a while."

Her eyes were sore. She glanced around, noting the screened hospital bed, and decided she was in the emergency room. She was incredibly tired. When she tried to speak, her voice was an unintelligible scratchy whisper.

The doctor said, "You've got a couple of people waiting to see you. I'll send them in."

Her mouth formed the word *Will*, but it wasn't Will who came around the screen to her bedside.

The Misses Munro peered at her anxiously, identical robin's egg blue eyes expressing their concern. "Oh, my dear, we were so worried about you. But the doctor says you're all right. Your friend Will and Cosmo are here too. Cosmo broke his ankle, but Will is fine, a few grazes on his hands and smoke inhalation, nothing serious."

Her sister added, "And the winds are dropping. The fire fighters hope to have the blaze contained by morning."

"Anders?" Alex tried to ask, but the word came out as a cough.

One of the misses Munro seemed to understand. "He's in a private room. He's quite shaken up, of course, and the doctors want to keep him here at least overnight." She blushed prettily. "After that he's coming home with us."

"Now, now, miss," her sister chided. "Don't give Alex the wrong idea. We're simply going to take care of him."

"Just as one of us should have forty years ago," her sister replied tartly. "But we let people tell us that he was . . . unsuitable for us. How very foolish we were. What a lot of time we wasted. Alex, dear, never let your head rule your heart, it's as much a mistake today as it was then."

Alex nodded, suddenly feeling very, very sleepy. Miss Munro murmured, "The doctor said she should rest, dear, perhaps we should go."

There were several things Alex wanted to say, not least of which was to ask that they send Will to her, but all at once she was floating down a long dimly-lit hall toward a flickering light, far off in the distance. There was a shadow in front of the light and she thought perhaps it was Will, but he vanished before she reached him. It's all right, she thought, I'm just dreaming, he's only a few feet away from me in the hospital emergency room.

Alex didn't trust herself to open the letter Will had left for her until after she checked out of the hospital the following morning.

Incredible as it was, it seemed that she had slept through the night. Nervous exhaustion, the doctor explained, as well as the effects of smoke inhalation.

She couldn't believe that Will had left without seeing her, even though she remembered that he'd said he had to continue the promotion tour today.

"He didn't want to disturb you," the receptionist explained, "and so he left you this letter."

Alex's car, smoke-grimed, was parked in the hospital lot. She sat in the driver's seat and ripped open Will's letter.

"*My Dear Alex,*" she read.

Sorry we never got to keep our dinner date. Just as well, perhaps, since candlelight and wine and being with you seem to bring out the beast in me and no doubt we'd have ended up making love—and I'm not sure I can stand any more physical intimacy that isn't combined with emotional intimacy. I was going to try to tell you that during dinner. But I was afraid I might start begging and that would turn you off even more than my lack of social credentials.

You've made your position pretty clear: you want to remain in Sand Point and continue with your practice. Of necessity, that means adhering to a set of social standards, mores, what-have-you that I find impossible to live with. I can never settle in Sand Point. And that seems to be that. I have no right to ask you to give up your dream.

So I suppose it's better to call it quits now, before we get in any deeper. When Meggie and the pups are able to travel, would you mind seeing that they arrive at the undernoted address safely?

I'll never forget you, Alex."

It was signed simply "Will."

Alex sat in the car for a full five minutes, staring at the letter in her hand. Every detail of every moment she had shared with him came rushing back to torment her. She replayed scenes in her mind until she couldn't stand the exquisite agony of remembering any longer and put her head down on the steering wheel and wept.

At last she turned the key in the ignition. She drove with reckless speed to the pet hospital, anxious to get to pen and paper and write a letter of her own.

Alex peered at the street name. Royal Vista Drive. That was the address to which she'd been directed to deliver Meggie, and the address to which she'd sent her reply to Will's letter.

In the back seat, Meggie began to bark excitedly. Her five-week-old puppies, safely housed in carrying cages, whimpered too, anxious for the long drive to be over. Evidently Meggie recognized her surroundings. She must have been here before. The house probably belonged to a friend of Will's.

Whoever that friend was, he might have forwarded her letter on to Will who surely couldn't have ignored it for all of these weeks, had he received it.

Royal Vista Drive was wide, tree-lined, with spacious houses surrounded by manicured lawns. Each house individual, different from its neighbors. In this expensive suburb, adjacent to the marina, Alex guessed the homes were at least in the million-dollar class. Especially since on one side of the street the homes were built along a backwater that led to the bay. Alex caught a glimpse of sleek white yachts moored at the owners' back doors.

The house she was seeking was one of the ones with its own boat mooring. Leaving the dogs in the car, parked on a circular driveway, she approached with some trepidation a handsome pair of carved oak double doors.

What if her postcard announcing her arrival with Meggie had not been received? She had asked that someone call to advise her if it were not convenient for her to bring the dogs today, but now she wished she'd asked for some confirmation.

Not knowing the name of the owner of the house she had simply addressed both letter and postcard to Will O'Keefe c/o the address she'd been given on Royal Vista Drive.

A young woman wearing a brief white bikini and a dark tan opened the door. "Hi, you must be Doctor Aimes, judging by the barking coming from your car. I'm Cindy, the house-sitter. Hey, let's go see the puppies."

Cindy ran lightly down the sloping path to the driveway, opened the car door and was instantly engulfed by an enthusiastic Golden Retriever. Alex watched as they rolled together on the lawn, Cindy laughing and protesting.

House-sitter? That meant the owners of the house were away. Cindy had no doubt read her postcard and decided to just let her bring the dogs. Unsure how to proceed, Alex walked down to the car.

After a few minutes Cindy extricated herself from

Meggie, stood up and went to look at the puppies. "Oh, my God, I've never seen anything so adorable!" She exclaimed in delight.

Alex smiled. "Aren't they beautiful? Everyone who sees them wants one."

"Let's get them into the house. There's an inner atrium where we can put them until they're housebroken. It connects to the garage so they can sleep in there." She picked up one of the carriers and Alex took another and followed.

Meggie rushed ahead of them and seemed to know her way to the atrium.

Over her shoulder Cindy said, "I was hoping Mr. O'Keefe would be here before you arrived, but I guess his plane must be late."

"You're expecting him to come here today?" Alex felt a rush of inner turbulence.

"Uh huh. Oh, hey, listen, I'm sorry I couldn't forward your letter to him, but I lost his itinerary. I thought maybe he'd call, but he hates making telephone calls."

"Yes, I know," Alex murmured, placing the carrier down on the brick floor of the atrium, and releasing a red-gold bundle of energy who wrapped himself around her leg.

"He had to go to England. I guess you knew that? His book was published there and got some sort of award and his British publishers wanted him to appear on some TV shows."

"No, I didn't know," Alex said, as Cindy let the other puppy out. So Will hadn't received her letter. Well, at least that explained why she hadn't had a reply.

Half an hour later the puppies and Meggie were installed in their new home and duly fed, and Cindy invited Alex to share a cold drink with her. They went into a beautifully appointed kitchen and Cindy poured iced tea into tall glasses. "What say we take it out onto the deck? I just love sitting out there and looking at all the boats go by. Especially the sailboats."

Halfway across a wooden deck Alex stopped short, the frosty glass almost slipping from her hand.

There was a large sailboat, white paint gleaming in the sun, moored to the rear of the house. But it was another boat, battered, weather-beaten, as disreputable-looking a scow as ever sailed the seas, that made Alex's heart start to beat faster. *Will's boat was tied up to the dock too.*

After her heart slowed its mad gallop, she realized that he had to leave his things somewhere; logically a friend who would take care of his dog would have no objection to sharing his mooring with Will's boat.

The two boats certainly looked incongruous, side by side. It made her reflect, sadly, about the haves and have-nots of the world. She sat on a deck chair beside Cindy and sipped her iced tea as Meggie prowled the deck, sniffing and examining large clay pots spilling geraniums. Her puppies were all sound asleep in their new bed in the garage.

There was a dog-door from garage to atrium, but Alex saw no sign that the owners of the house presently owned their own pet.

After a while Cindy glanced at her watch. "Oh, hey, listen, I've got to run. I've got a date. Would you mind doing me a huge favor and hanging around until either Will or Mrs. Endicott gets here? She's coming back from Hawaii, in fact she should be on her way from the airport now."

"I'd be glad to," Alex said, thinking that wild horses

wouldn't get her out of there if there was a chance of seeing Will. She assumed Mrs. Endicott was the owner of the house, and said a silent prayer that she wouldn't prove to be a gorgeous young widow with designs on Will.

After Cindy left, Alex prowled restlessly, wishing she'd dressed in something more attractive than a pair of serviceable slacks and rather severely tailored shirt.

Several rooms opened to the deck by means of large sliding glass doors and inside the house she could see a pleasant mixture of antique and contemporary furniture and, in one curio cabinet, a collection of beautiful jade. Mrs. Endicott had good taste. Everything in the house blended in perfect harmony. *Why had there been no mention of a Mr. Endicott?*

Before that question could plague her any further, the phone rang inside the house. Alex hesitated, reluctant to answer someone else's phone. But Cindy was gone and wasn't she, Alex, temporarily house-sitting? What if it were Mrs. Endicott, or Will needing a ride from the airport?

Alex answered the phone on the sixth ring. A woman's voice, surprised, asked, "Cindy?" Alex explained the situation and the woman said, "Oh, I see. I'm Mrs. Endicott. My plane was late and I just landed. It'll take me an hour to get there. Mr. O'Keefe should be arriving any time, so if you want to leave . . ."

"I'll wait until he arrives," Alex said quickly. "I have some instructions about the puppies." Liar, she thought, all you have on your mind is grabbing Will and never letting go of him again.

Moments after replacing the receiver, Alex heard a key

in the front door and Meggie gave a yelp of delight and went tearing into the entry hall. Alex followed. Will had placed a suitcase down on the floor and now bent to hug Meggie.

Their eyes met over the top of the dog's golden head. Will said softly, "I hoped you'd bring her yourself. I really wanted to be here when you arrived, but transatlantic flights . . ." His voice trailed off and he straightened up, came toward her with his arms outstretched.

The next moment she was enclosed by those powerful, loving arms and she felt a long shudder run through her body in the instant before his mouth claimed hers in a kiss that was pure magic. In the touch of his lips and tongue was both the heartache of their absence from one another and joy in their reunion.

For a long time neither spoke. They clung together, running hands over backs, shoulders, thighs, kissing, nibbling, gazing at one another in astonished recognition of the force of their love.

At last Will released her lips and said, "That letter I sent you—I guess it was a cry of despair. I didn't know how to tell you how much I love you, need you to be with me. I wanted to ask you to marry me, but I was afraid you'd say no, so, like a fool, I had to say goodbye instead."

"Oh, Will, what blind fools we've been! I wrote you a letter too. I think perhaps it's waiting for you with that stack of mail on the table over there. Will you read it now?"

"If it's a Dear John . . ." he said, only half-joking.

"Never," she said quickly.

He released her reluctantly, planted another kiss on her lips, and went to the table. Her letter was quickly found among the pile of bills and business letters, no doubt addressed to the Endicotts—or at least, Mrs. Endicott.

Will held the envelope next to his heart as he slipped his arm around her waist and led her into the living room. They sat side by side on a huge couch that wrapped around two walls.

Alex knew every word he was reading, she'd re-written the letter several times.

My Darling Will, she'd written, *If all that's between you and me being together is my stubborn wish to make a go of my practice in Sand Point then I say to hell with Sand Point. I've pulled my practice back out of the doldrums now and no one can say I'm leaving with my tail between my legs. In fact, I believe I could sell the practice for almost what I paid for it.*

I do need to put down roots somewhere and build another practice though. If you can compromise your lifestyle enough to do that, you name the place. You're more important to me than anyone, or anything else. I love you, Will. Alex.

P.S. Red Baron says he'll die of a broken heart if you take his wife away from him.

Will smilingly folded up the letter and wrapped his arms around her. He buried his face in her hair and said, "Alex, Alex. If I might be permitted to use the oldest— truest—cliché on earth . . . you've just made me the happiest man alive. I love you so much, so much I was afraid to try to put it into words because they'd be so inadequate."

"I love you too—and yes, I'll marry you, quickly, before you change your mind."

"No chance!" He reached for the buttons on her blouse.

Laughing, they undressed each other, and forgetful of their surroundings, came together in a frenzy of need. They made love on the couch, then rolled to the floor, still locked together, and made love again.

It seemed a long time later that Alex, nestled in the curve of Will's arm, her head on his chest, aroused herself from her rosy afterglow and said, "Oh, my God. What if Mrs. Endicott finds us like this?"

Will stroked her hair with a tender touch. "She would discreetly withdraw to the kitchen."

"She would? Oh, Will, promise me she'll turn out to be a sweet old soul with blue hair!"

"A sweet old soul yes, but with salt and pepper hair. What did you think, that I'd hire a housekeeper who looked like Cindy?"

Alex sat up, looked down at him. "You . . . hire a housekeeper? Mrs. Endicott is *your* housekeeper?"

"Yes, didn't Cindy tell you?"

Alex shook her head, as other unbelievable possibilities took shape. "Then this house . . ."

"Mine."

"And that white yacht moored out there . . ."

"Also mine."

"But, I thought . . . that battered old boat out there, that you were living in—"

Will smiled, "That's mine too. I bought it to use as living quarters for the last part of the research for my book. I was exploring all of the beach communities of the West Coast, from Venice and the poorer beach towns near the Mexican border to super-rich havens like Sand

Point and Newport Beach. By the time I was ready for the beach research, I'd had enough of flea-bitten digs, abandoned houses, cardboard boxes under freeway bridges and sleeping on the bare ground."

"Research. You lived like the people you were researching," Alex said, dazed.

"Actually, by the time I reached Sand Point, the book was finished, but I'd been commissioned to do a couple of magazine articles. Yes, I dressed like them, lived like them. I couldn't have brought any real authenticity to my writing if I'd stayed here. I sent Mrs. Endicott on a well-earned vacation to her daughter's family in Hawaii, hired Cindy to house-sit and stripped myself of everything of value, including money. I decided I'd get by as the wanderers do."

"You might have told me," Alex said.

"Would it have made a difference to you? I thought our only problem was that I couldn't abide Sand Point and you wanted to stay there."

He simply doesn't care about possessions, she thought. It never occurred to him to offer anything but himself. And, come to think of it, what else do any of us have that really matters?

"If you're thinking that this house, the yacht, seems to contradict all I wrote, I suppose in a way it does. But I did earn all of this. Oh, not with my writing, but years ago I crewed on a yacht and invented a new kind of sailing boat, which made me a lot of money. Enough that I was able to indulge my compulsion to write. I must admit that a few times during my research I cheated and tapped my bank account—like when I had to come up with a hundred bucks to get into Amelia Barrington's shindig."

The difference with his house, his neighborhood, she

thought, was that it was part of the vast hodge-podge of a metropolitan city, where every kind of neighborhood from poor to rich existed side by side. Where it was possible to move up, if one had the means, to a better house, a more affluent area. In Sand Point, that wasn't possible. All but the super-rich were excluded. She did see his point.

"If this house isn't what you had in mind, if you'd be more comfortable somewhere else," Will said, picking up her hand and bringing her fingers to his lips, "just say the word. We'll sell up and go wherever you like. All I need is my typewriter and Meggie."

Alex kissed the hand that held hers and murmured, "Wait till Red Baron sees his new quarters!"

An epic novel of exotic rituals
and the lure of the Upper Amazon

THE TAKERS
RIVER OF GOLD

JERRY AND S.A. AHERN

THE TAKERS are the intrepid Josh Culhane and the seductive Mary Mulrooney. These two adventurers launch an incredible journey into the Brazilian rain forest. Far upriver, the jungle yields its deepest secret—the lost city of the Amazon warrior women!

THE TAKERS series is making publishing history. Awarded *The Romantic Times* first prize for High Adventure in 1984, the opening book in the series was hailed by *The Romantic Times* as "the next trend in romance writing and reading. Highly recommended!"

Jerry and S.A. Ahern have never been better!

TAK–3

For the woman who expects a little more out of love, get Silhouette Special Edition.

Take 4 books free—no strings attached.

If you yearn to experience more passion and pleasure in your romance reading ... to share even the most private moments of romance and sensual love between spirited heroines and their ardent lovers, then Silhouette Special Edition has everything you've been looking for.

Get 6 books each month before they are available anywhere else!

Act now and we'll send you four exciting Silhouette Special Edition romance novels. They're our gift to introduce you to our convenient home subscription service. Every month, we'll send you six new passion-filled Special Edition books. Look them over for 15 days. If you keep them, pay just $11.70 for all six. Or return them at no charge.

We'll mail your books to you *two full months before they are available* anywhere else. Plus, with every shipment, you'll receive the Silhouette Books Newsletter absolutely free. *And with Silhouette Special Edition there are never any shipping or handling charges.*

Mail the coupon today to get your four free books — and more romance than you ever bargained for.

Silhouette Special Edition is a service mark and a registered trademark.